Prophet Motive

HEDGEWITCH FOR HIRE – BOOK 8

CHRISTINE POPE

PROPHET MOTIVE

Copyright © 2022 by Christine Pope

ISBN: 978-1-946435-58-3

Published by Dark Valentine Press

Cover design by Lou Harper

Ebook formatting by Indie Author Services

Don't miss out on any of Christine's new releases—sign up for her newsletter today!

Call to Glory

MY FRIEND JOSIE WOODROW—GLOBE, Arizona's busiest real estate agent...and its newly minted mayor, as she'd just been sworn in the week before—had been standing in front of my shop and staring at the sign above the door for so long that I felt compelled to come outside to see what could possibly be so fascinating about the thing.

"What's up?" I asked, once I'd deduced that the Once in a Blue Moon sign was in the proper position and didn't appear to have been vandalized or otherwise compromised.

She gave a halfway guilty start, and then offered me a tentative smile that looked very unlike her. Say what you want on the subject of Josie Woodrow, but no one could ever accuse her of being shy and retiring.

"Oh, probably nothing," she replied with one of her patented airy hand waves, the sort of gesture that told me whatever was going on with her, it was much more than just "nothing." Because Thanksgiving was now less than two weeks away, she wore a rust-colored blazer that went well with her coppery-red hair, and an enameled autumn leaf pin glinted from her lapel. As usual, she had on sensible heels that added a couple of inches to her barely five-foot-two height, and the way her jacket strained to contain her plump form told me she'd probably added a few pounds over the past month or so, even if she was doing her best to ignore that unwelcome fact.

"You seem awfully interested in my sign for it to be 'nothing,'" I said, and she let out a sigh.

Once again, she glanced up at the rectangular piece of wood. It had the name of the shop painted on it in dark blue vaguely Art Nouveau lettering and an illustration of a round blue moon with the crescent on its right side picked out in white paint. My friend Hazel Marr had painted it for me, just as she'd painted the gorgeous mural of constellations and the moon on the ceiling of the store.

Anyway, there was nothing about the sign that should have aroused Josie's interest, especially since it had been hanging above the door to my shop for the past year and a half, and had never attracted any particular attention before now.

"I'm just hoping it won't offend anyone," she said, and I lifted an eyebrow.

"'Offend who'?" I asked, wondering where that particular notion could have come from. "How in the world could my shop sign offend anyone?"

It seemed a simple enough question to me. While there were definitely people in town who weren't exactly fans of my New Age store—and even less thrilled that the woman running it was a self-professed witch—the sign itself certainly wasn't anything that should have invoked even the most narrow-minded person's ire. After all, it wasn't as though I'd had Hazel paint a witch riding a broomstick superimposed on the moon or anything close to that.

Once again, Josie hesitated. Then she gathered a breath, as if realizing that she needed to simply come right out and answer me directly.

"I didn't want to say anything until it was a done deal," she told me. "But since we just finalized the contract, I figure you should be the first to know that the Life Springs Church is going to have one of their prayer gatherings here in town on the weekend of the nineteenth and twentieth."

This revelation didn't have the impact she'd probably hoped it would, probably because I'd never even heard of the Life Springs Church. Not so surprising, I supposed, since I barely kept up with the doings of the local Methodist and Catholic churches here in Globe, and so couldn't be bothered to pay attention to an organization that clearly wasn't local.

My expression must have been one of mystification, because Josie hurried to add, "Oh, they're very big. Pastor Aaron has one of the largest congregations west of the Mississippi."

Which made me wonder why he'd chosen tiny little Globe as the site of his latest tent revival meeting, or whatever this gathering was supposed to be. Wouldn't Phoenix or one of its suburbs have been a more likely location?

"So, he's a TV preacher," I said, hoping I didn't sound too judgmental.

"Well, yes," Josie replied. She now looked a little uncomfortable, as though she'd wondered privately whether inviting such an organization to hold a meeting in her hometown might be a betrayal of her fierce loyalty to the local Methodist church. But then she hastened to add, "I've read that Life Spring Church contributes a huge amount of money to various charities, and they do many more good works. We should be honored that they're coming here to Globe."

Her tone was almost defensive, which made me slant a glance up at the shop sign again. Now that I had a bit more context, I thought I could see where her concern about Once in a Blue Moon might be coming from.

"And you're worried about what they're going to think when they figure out there's a New Age shop downtown," I said.

"Well, 'worried' is putting it a bit too strongly," she replied at once, sounding a little less prickly now that she'd realized I probably wasn't going to be offended by her concerns. "But I don't want them to get the wrong impression."

"What, that Globe's overrun with pagans?" I returned with a grin. Over the years, I'd learned not to get too upset by some people's reactions to my own paganism, so by this point, I'd earned enough detachment to be mostly amused by the whole thing.

Now Josie looked truly flustered. "No, of course not. I mean, it's very clear that most of the people here are good Christians." She stopped there, then quickly went on, "Not that you're not a very good person, Selena, but—"

My grin only broadened. "But I'm definitely not Christian. Fair enough." I paused and sent a glance at the shop's picture window. The display for November consisted of as many warm-toned crystal specimens as I could scrounge from my inventory, tastefully accented with branches of silk autumn leaves. Honestly, someone walking by and giving the place only a cursory glance would probably think my store was some kind of mineral emporium, rather than a New Age shop. Still smiling a little, I said, "I think it's going to be fine."

She glanced past me to take a look at the shop window for herself and seemed to relax slightly. "You're probably right. It's just—we've never had an event of this size take place in Globe before."

Quite possibly not. My adopted hometown was the kind of place that tended to get overlooked, despite being the county seat. But because we had only a little more than seven thousand residents, we were seen mainly as a wide spot in the road for people traveling between Payson and Phoenix.

True, we'd had a film crew come through to film the ill-fated *Monster Hunt* series—whose host managed to get himself murdered right here in town—and we'd been the site of Instagram witch Lilith Black's solstice festival more than a year ago, but otherwise, we weren't exactly the sort of place that tended to attract much notice.

And I liked it that way. After spending most of my existence in busy, overcrowded Southern California, I was more than happy to live life at a much slower pace.

"Where is this Life Springs Church even going to hold their revival?" I asked, honestly curious. It wasn't as if Globe was exactly over-flowing with the sorts of locations that could host a gathering of what sounded as though it could be thousands of people.

"Oh, they're going to have the event at Memorial Park," Josie responded, now clearly relieved that I was inquiring about logistics rather than worrying about whether I was going to offend any of the people coming to town for the gathering. "It's the only space on city prop-erty that's big enough."

Right. The town hosted its annual Fourth of July festival at the park, as well as a few smaller events, but for the rest of the time, it stood empty except for the usual round of dog-walkers and kids who liked to hang out to vape some-place where their parents couldn't catch them. If Josie had figured out a way to have the park bring in some much-needed funds for the city, then more power to her.

And as for why the higher-ups at Life

Springs had decided to hold such an event the weekend before Thanksgiving, I had no idea, but I assumed they must have their reasons.

It was none of my business, anyway. Or at any rate, I was fully prepared to stay out of their business…as long as they stayed out of mine.

"Well, that sounds like a good plan," I said. "I'll be interested to hear how it all goes."

She nodded, a smile of her own touching her lips. Probably, she was relieved I hadn't taken offense at her fears that my store might send the wrong message about Globe.

"Oh, it should be wonderful for the town," she said. "But I won't keep you any longer. I'm sure you have oodles to do."

If only. Midweek days tended to be the slowest at the store, although business had begun to pick up lately as people started to focus on their holiday shopping.

"I need to check on Archie," I said, naming the man who'd once been a cursed cat but who had been working as my assistant at the store for the past six months, ever since he'd broken the curse that had kept him in feline form for some seventy-plus years. Some might have argued that Once in a Blue Moon wasn't really busy enough to require a second person working there, but I'd realized I needed to do something to keep him off the street...so to speak. "But thanks for dropping by."

Josie lifted a hand to say goodbye, then strode off briskly in the direction of her office, which was located about a block away. Her real estate office, that is, since, as mayor, she now also had an office at City Hall. However, since her business selling houses seemed to keep her far more occupied than running the town, she didn't appear to spend much time in the government building unless she was having some kind of meeting. I hadn't been present at any of those meetings, but I'd heard she had a grand time wielding her gavel.

I went back inside the store. Archie was over at the bookshelves at the far side of the shop, working on rearranging the volumes there so they were listed in alphabetical order by author in their overall subject groupings. No one had ever complained about a particular book being hard to find, but honestly, if the fiddly little task made him happy, I wasn't going to argue.

As usual, he looked like someone who'd stepped out of a J. Crew catalogue rather than a clerk in a small shop in a town most people had never heard of. His dark blond hair waved perfectly back from his high forehead, and he wore sharply creased khakis, a maroon sweater, and the shiniest loafers I'd ever seen.

"What did Josie want?" he asked.

Because Archie and Josie at best had a relationship of armed neutrality—I often thought of them as the irresistible force meeting the immovable object—I figured it was probably better not to pass along her worries that my store might offend the sensibilities of the people coming to Globe for Life Springs' tent revival.

"Oh, she just wanted to let me know about an event that's coming up the weekend before Thanksgiving," I said, doing my best to sound neutral. "Some televangelist is having a gathering here at Memorial Park. So that means there'll probably be more traffic, more people in the restaurants around here, that kind of thing."

The expression of disdain that flitted across his features as he absorbed this news heartened me a little. Archie and I had never discussed religion, but since he also hadn't joined any of the local churches since reassuming his human form, I had to believe he wasn't terribly devout.

"Sanctioned highway robbery," he said, his tone dripping with scorn. "Bilking innocent people out of money they can't afford to give."

I was a little surprised to hear him express his opinion so bluntly. Not that Archie Bradshaw was the sort of man to mince words, but still, I had no idea he'd harbored such strong opinions on the subject.

"Well, that's true about some televangelists," I responded, figuring I should try to be diplomatic. "I don't really know anything about Life Springs, though, so I suppose we should probably give them the benefit of the doubt."

"Hmph," Archie said, sounding so much like his former cat self that I wouldn't have been too surprised to see him sprouting some whiskers. He picked up a book from the pile on a stool nearby and slid it onto the shelf with unexpected vehemence.

Although I didn't do too much to probe into his personal life or his past history—mostly because I knew he'd shut me down as soon as I began to ask any leading questions—I couldn't help venturing, "This sounds personal, Archie."

His chin lifted. Without looking at me, he said, "It's possible that I had some…negative… interactions with members of the clergy back in the day. They didn't approve of me."

Ah. All right, that explained things a bit. Before he'd become a cat, Archie had been firmly convinced he was asexual, since he'd never experienced attraction to members of either sex. Once he met Victoria Parrish, however, the woman who'd planned my wedding to Calvin, it became clear to Archie that it wasn't precisely that he was asexual, only that he'd been waiting for the right person to come along…even though it had taken seventy-plus years.

Luckily for everyone involved, Victoria was just as attracted to Archie as he was to her, and they'd begun a long-distance courtship not too long after their first meeting. And clearly, things were getting serious, since she'd scaled back her wedding planning business so she could go back to school to get her interior design certification. She'd decided on getting just the certificate rather than a full-on bachelor's because it seemed obvious she wanted to switch careers as soon as possible, probably with an eye to relocating from Scottsdale to Globe.

Some might have asked why Archie, who didn't have a real career anymore thanks to being in a cat's body for more than seventy years, wasn't the one who was considering uprooting himself, but my conversations with Victoria had made it pretty clear that she was tired of the rat race and was only too ready to move someplace where she could live life at a slower pace. Since I'd done that exact same thing, she knew I could lend a sympathetic ear to hose discussions.

At any rate, I could read between the lines and guess that some members of the clergy back in Archie's day might have asked a few pointed questions about his perpetually single state. Their assumptions would have been dead wrong, of course, but I doubted anyone in the 1950s had even heard of a demisexual, let alone understood what it meant.

"Well, I don't think we'll have to deal with too many members of Life Springs Church," I assured him. "This isn't the kind of place where they'd be likely to hang out."

He sniffed. "Well, unless they decide to organize some sort of protest outside."

That thought hadn't even occurred to me, but I assumed it might be remotely possible. Still, since my general philosophy was not to borrow trouble, I just shrugged and said, "I'm sure they'll be so busy with attending the events their church has planned that they won't have time for protesting."

Even as I spoke, though, I realized I didn't really know that for sure. It wasn't as if I'd ever attended anything like the event that was going to take place in Memorial Park ten days from now. I sort of doubted a psychic fair was exactly the same thing as a tent revival.

But either Archie knew more than I did, or he was equally clueless but not going to admit his ignorance, because he only gave a shrug before reaching for another volume to set on the bookshelf. "I suppose we'll find out one way or another," he said.

I couldn't really argue with that comment. Because, like it or not, Life Springs Church and its true believers were going to descend on Globe in the very near future.

2

Outside Help

As happened about half the time these days, I left Archie to close up the shop so I could head home a little early. It wasn't as though he had much of a commute, since he'd moved into my old apartment over the store. He'd stayed at Hazel's Airbnb, which was actually the house he'd owned back in the day before he was turned into a cat, for some three weeks, but she hadn't wanted to sell the place, which would have been the simplest solution for Archie's housing dilemma. And because my apartment became vacant after I moved in with Calvin following our wedding, it seemed the most logical place to house the former cat.

To my surprise, though, Archie had been almost philosophical about the situation. "Yes, Hazel's house was my home once," he told me after I delivered the bad news that she didn't want to sell. "But it doesn't really feel that way anymore, not with how it's been decorated. And anyone I once knew who lived on that street has been dead a long time." He'd paused there and glanced upward at the apartment overhead, adding, "Really, the apartment feels just as much like home to me. I lived there for more than a year, after all."

I couldn't really argue with that observation, and so Archie had moved into the apartment, saving me the trouble of figuring out what to do with the place. Hazel had suggested that I use it for an Airbnb, just as she had with the little bungalow that had been her home until she moved in with Chuck Langdon, her fiancé, but I wasn't overly thrilled about that idea. The apartment was the first place I'd actually owned, the first home that had ever been completely mine, and I hadn't liked the idea of strangers using it as a casual way station and nothing more.

But I knew Archie would treat the cozy flat with the respect it deserved, and since I'd bought both the apartment and the shop for cash, it wasn't as though I needed to charge him rent to cover the cost of my mortgage. I could tell he wasn't completely thrilled about having to depend on my largesse—especially since I'd also given him a job that wasn't entirely necessary—but at least he hadn't argued about it too much. One disastrous attempt at subbing at the local high school had been enough to convince him that, even if he might have been a decent history teacher back in the 1950s, he just wasn't emotionally equipped to deal with twenty-first-century kids.

Since I'd left work a little early, it was fairly light out as I drove home. Even after six months, it still felt kind of strange to not simply walk upstairs to my former apartment and instead have to make a trek of about four miles to reach the lovely adobe home in the wilderness that Calvin and I shared. I also wasn't quite used to the Jeep Renegade we'd purchased to replace my old Beetle convertible, a car I'd gifted to Archie once I had my new wheels—and once I was sure he could handle driving a modern vehicle.

Change was the only real constant in the world, however, and so I told myself it wouldn't be too long before I was completely adjusted to my new normal and had begun to forget what life was like back when I was just Selena Marx and not Calvin Standingbear's wife.

I hadn't changed my name, though. Not too long after we were engaged, I'd told Calvin that, while I loved him to the moon and back, I wasn't ready to completely leave Selena Marx behind. And he, being the amazing soul that he was, had only smiled at me and told me he understood, that Marx was a lot easier to deal with than his own family name.

Because he'd put in an early shift that day, his big white tribal police–issue Durango was sitting in the driveway as I pulled up. The house had a two-car garage, but it was filled with the usual flotsam and jetsam that always seemed to accumulate in a place where someone had lived for a while. More than once, I'd gently hinted that we could get a storage unit in town for all his stuff and that I'd really like to be able to park my brand-new SUV inside, but so far, he hadn't gone along with the scheme.

The situation was mildly annoying but not enough of an irritation for me to make a big deal about his stubbornness, so I did the same thing I'd been doing for the past six months, which was to pull into the driveway next to Calvin's Durango and turn off the engine. Whether I'd be quite so cheery about the whole thing when and if we got some actual snow remained to be seen, but in the meantime, it seemed better to just let it go.

As soon as I opened the front door, my little chihuahua mix Sadie was there, tail wagging furiously. I'd found her hiding under my car nearly six months earlier and brought her home with me, and she'd become a part of the family immediately. Yes, I'd done my due diligence and checked with the local vet to make sure she wasn't microchipped, and I'd hung flyers and checked on every single lost dog Facebook group and website I could think of.

But no one claimed her or posted anything about a missing dog that matched her description—much to my relief—and soon enough, it was hard to imagine my life without her. Doggy DNA testing had shown her to be a chihuahua/papillon mix, which explained her oversized ears and general adorableness. She was such a well-behaved little dog that I sometimes brought her to work with me, but I'd left her at the house today because I knew Calvin would be home a little after three, and so she wouldn't have to be alone for a terribly long amount of time.

I reached down to pet her and assure her she was the cutest dog in the world, and then went in search of my husband, with Sadie trotting along at my heels.

He was sitting at the dining room table as I came in, laptop open in front of him and a faint frown creasing his level black brows. However, his expression cleared as soon as he saw me and my canine companion, and he smiled.

"Hey, hon."

"Hey, yourself," I said, then came over and planted a kiss on top of his shining black head. As usual, he had his long, raven-hued tresses pulled back into a severe ponytail, but since I knew what that gorgeous hair looked like when he let it down, I didn't mind too much that he almost always wore it so confined. My gaze shifted to his laptop, a small MacBook Air that always looked somewhat dwarfed by his tall frame and broad shoulders. "What're you working on?"

"Crowd control proposal for an event on the nineteenth," he responded.

"The Life Springs Church event?" I asked, and he lifted a surprised eyebrow.

"How'd you know about that?"

"Josie," I said briefly as I settled myself in the chair next to his. Immediately, Sadie sat down next to me, tail still wagging. She knew that Calvin and I liked to catch up on each other's days before I started prepping dinner, so she was ready to wait for as long as necessary.

A sort of weary amusement gleamed in his dark eyes. "I should have known Josie would spill the beans," he replied.

"They're asking the San Ramon tribal police for security support?" I asked then. I hadn't thought Calvin's force would get involved in an event that was taking place inside Globe's town limits—Chief Henry Lewis's territory—but I didn't see any other reason why Calvin would be spending time on such a proposal.

"Yes," Calvin said. "Chelsea Haven—I guess she's the pastor's right-hand woman—reached out to me specifically. She said they'll have some private security but also wanted to see if anyone on the tribe's police force wanted to moonlight. I guess they want to make sure they're not taking anyone away from Henry's detail."

"But they think it's okay to leave the tribal police short-staffed?" I asked, my tone a little more acerbic than I'd intended.

Calvin shrugged and closed his laptop. "Well, it's not like we have much to keep ourselves occupied most of the time. To be honest, I could probably get by with fewer deputies if I had to, but the tribal elders determine the size of our police force, and I figure they probably think it's better to have as many good-paying jobs for our people as possible."

Well, I couldn't really argue with that stance. The San Ramon Apache tended to keep to themselves—probably because they couldn't allow the outside world to ever learn they were actually coyote shifters—but, like many Native American tribes, they weren't exactly rolling in dough. The casino they owned just past Globe's eastern border brought in what seemed to be a decent chunk of money, and many of them were involved in ranching one way or another, and yet many of the members of the tribe appeared to just scrape by. Having as many deputies as they could on the police force made a lot of sense.

"Anyway," Calvin went on, "I told Ms. Haven that I should probably be able to get five or six deputies who're willing to work her event. I was just going over the specs she gave me—the proposed layout of the facilities, the size of the crowds they're expecting to have—before I gave her a firm answer. But what I've seen so far tells me it should be doable."

"And you're not worried about stepping on Henry's toes?" I asked.

The faintest ghost of a grimace touched Calvin's mouth before he shook his head. "Not too much. I mean, he'll probably get pissed about it, but there's really not much he can do. My deputies will be working as private security and not in their capacity as members of the San Ramon tribal police, so it's not as if we're dealing with some kind of jurisdiction issue here."

On paper, no. But considering that Calvin and Henry's relationship was prickly at best, I was sure that Globe's police chief would figure out some way to give my husband grief over the situation.

"It seems like the Life Springs people are being pretty last-minute about all this," I remarked. Not that I could pretend to have much experience planning large-scale events—other than my own disastrous solstice observation more than a year before, one that Instagram witch Lilith Black had managed to effectively sabotage—but still, ten days didn't seem like a huge chunk of time to organize a gathering that was sure to attract at least a thousand people, maybe more.

Calvin gave a resigned lift of his shoulders. "I was thinking that, too, but it sounds like they were supposed to hold the event somewhere in Mesa and the location fell through, for whatever reason. That was why Chelsea Haven reached out to Josie—she'd heard of Globe, and since we're just a little more than an hour away from Mesa and a lot of their people already had hotel reservations there, she was hoping we could hold the event here."

"There wasn't anywhere closer?" I asked, thinking that an hour-plus drive was still a pretty long commute. After all, it wasn't as though Mesa was the only Phoenix suburb where the church could hold its tent revival.

"Not according to Ms. Haven," Calvin

replied. "I didn't press her for details or anything, but I got the impression that she tried several other venues but couldn't find anywhere at such late notice."

I supposed that made sense. Any location that could accommodate that many people was probably booked out months in advance.

Whereas Memorial Park sat largely unused for most of the year. I had a feeling the local merchants wouldn't be too thrilled to learn that a lot of the event's attendees were staying at hotels more than an hour away and so might not be spending as much money in Globe as we all would have liked. On the other hand, even though Josie hadn't given me any exact details, I got the impression the church was paying enough for the privilege of using the park that it wasn't as though we'd all be walking away empty-handed from this.

And honestly, I was sort of relieved my little hometown wouldn't be overrun with Life Springs devotees twenty-four/seven. It probably wasn't very enlightened of me, but after hearing Josie's worries about whether my innocuous little shop might offend some of them, I was just fine with the event's attendees not being around very much.

"Well, then," I said briskly, "I'll leave you to it. I need to get dinner started anyway."

Calvin offered me a grateful smile, then took my hand and pulled me toward him so he could give me a delayed kiss on the lips. "Do you have any idea how much I love you?"

"Mmm…maybe," I returned with a grin. "But you can prove it to me later."

He returned my smile, then reopened his laptop. With Sadie trotting along at my feet, I headed off to the kitchen to start putting together that evening's chicken cacciatore.

As far as I could tell, the Life Springs Church gathering would be a blip on Globe's radar and nothing more. Which was fine by me, because Calvin and I would be hosting Thanksgiving dinner for as much of his family as would fit into the house—plus Archie and Victoria, since Archie really didn't have anywhere else to go, and from what I could tell, Victoria's family was all located out of state—and I had plenty of other things to occupy my mind.

After all, everything had been blessedly quiet these past six months, and I saw no reason why holding a church revival here in town would do anything to upset our wonderfully serene world.

3

Free Pass

THE NEXT WEEK SEEMED TO FLY BY. YES, THERE was an undercurrent of excitement in the town, just because quiet little Globe didn't often host the kind of events that drew people from all over the state...and maybe even farther away. Besides, getting a visit from a semi-celebrity like Aaron Galloway, whose television ministry boasted millions of viewers every week, was pretty much the icing on the cake.

I didn't see very much of Josie, which I supposed was to be expected. Between her mayoral duties and her successful real estate business, she was already working crazy hours, and the impending arrival of the Life Springs Church delegation ate up even more of her time. One might have wondered if the Globe real estate market was really all that hot, but she did seem to have a continuous stream of listings to manage, even if some of those listings were located as far away as Apache Junction.

Archie seemed singularly unimpressed by the impending arrival of the Life Springs contingent. No big surprise there, either, but at least Victoria was planning to come out for the weekend so they could spend some time together, and her presence should keep him pretty well occupied. Those weekend visits had become a regular occurrence, and I had a feeling I wasn't the only one who'd noticed her red Mercedes SUV parked in back of the building for the entire forty-eight hours she was here in Globe.

Apparently Archie, who'd always seemed prim and proper to the extreme, had decided to embrace at least a few of the twenty-first century's more relaxed standards. I was glad for him, even as I wondered if he ever planned to tell his girlfriend the truth about himself. So far, he'd been maintaining the fiction that he was a cousin of mine from California, but I had to wonder how long Victoria would accept that admittedly thin story.

Then again, it was probably easier to believe he was my cousin, living off a modest inheritance while helping out at the shop, than trying to accept that he'd spent the past seventy-plus years in the body of a smoke-gray cat.

On Friday morning, a series of flatbed trucks made their way along Broad Street toward Memorial Park, carrying all the infrastructure for the huge circus-style tent that was going to be erected in the middle of the field. And while I'd done my best to seem blasé about Life Springs Church coming to visit our little town, I suggested to Archie that we close up early that afternoon so we could wander down to the park and watch the pavilion being set up.

I'd halfway expected him to shoot down my proposal and tell me he had absolutely no interest in acting like a silly tourist, but instead he shrugged and replied, "Why not? I doubt we're going to get many customers with that sort of distraction going on only a few blocks away."

True, things had been pretty dead for a Friday afternoon, especially when you considered how holiday shopping in general had picked up over the past week or so. If I'd needed the income from the store to support myself, I might have been more concerned about the lack of shoppers, but since my entirely unexpected inheritance from Lucien Dumond, the former head of the Greater Los Angeles Necromancers' Guild, more than a year and a half ago had ensured I'd never need to worry about money ever again, it only seemed as though the unnaturally quiet afternoon was giving Archie and me the perfect excuse to slip away early.

So we locked up the store and headed out, Sadie tugging at her leash as we made our way along the sidewalk. I'd brought her to work that day because Calvin would be at the station until nine and I didn't want to leave her alone for so many hours. Yes, she was a very well-behaved dog and had never had an accident in the house even once, but I didn't see any reason to tempt fate. Besides, when she was with me at work, she knew to go back to her bed behind the counter whenever we had a customer come in — even though she loved people and usually wanted to meet everyone — and so her presence at the store was very low-key.

It was a beautiful late autumn day, the trees now mostly bare except for a few cottonwoods, which always seemed to be some of the last to drop their golden leaves. The air had a definite bite to it without being actually cold, and a few puffy white clouds drifted their way across the deep sapphire skies. Maybe it would have been even better to have Calvin at my side, but Archie had unexpectedly turned out to be one of my best friends, someone who already knew all about my odd angles and quirks, thanks to living with me in cat form for more than a year.

We clearly weren't the only people who'd had the same idea to go rubbernecking, because I spied several small groups converging on Memorial Park as we grew closer. Among them was Joyce Lewis, Chief Lewis's wife, who waved at me and Archie when we approached.

"It's very exciting, isn't it?" she said once we were close enough. She was there with her bestie Lynda Holt, who offered me a friendly smile and Archie a glance that was almost predatory. Yes, it was pretty clear to everyone who was paying even the barest attention that he was seriously involved with Victoria Parrish, but Lynda had gotten divorced only a few months earlier and now appeared to be on the prowl for any eligible males in the vicinity.

Being Archie, though, he didn't appear to notice anything strange about the way Lynda looked at him. One eyebrow lifted at a slightly sarcastic angle as he told Joyce, "I don't know about 'exciting.' It seems like a lot of sound and fury and not much else."

She sent him a look that was almost shocked. "You don't think it's important for a church to spread the word?"

I figured I'd better step in before things got too uncomfortable. Joyce Lewis was one of the kindest people I knew—I still couldn't figure out how she and crotchety Henry had managed to stay together for nearly thirty years—but she was also a devout churchgoer, someone who overlooked my pagan status because she liked me as a person. Archie, however, was more of an unknown quantity. He'd never once gone to church but also clearly didn't subscribe to any of my esoteric beliefs. I'd introduced him to everyone as my cousin from California, thus explaining why I'd given him my apartment to live in and why he was working at the store, and so I got the impression that a lot of the people in Globe expected him to be a Tarot-reading, crystal-ball-consulting practitioner like I was.

Nothing could be further from the truth—so far, it seemed as though Archie didn't believe in much of anything except his adoration for Victoria Parrish—but I also didn't see the harm in a little obfuscation.

"Oh, we're not really churchy people," I said hastily, which was nothing more than the truth. "But I have to admit I'm curious to see how all this goes together."

Luckily, Joyce wasn't the proselytizing type, so she appeared content to let the matter go. "Me too," she replied. "I've never watched any of Pastor Galloway's shows, but I kind of want to attend one of his services. Do you think there are any tickets still available?"

I had absolutely no idea. All the talk had made it sound as though the Life Springs Church was expecting a good-sized crowd, but was that expectation based on attendance at past events or actual advance ticket sales?

"I'm not sure," I said. "I suppose you could go to the Life Springs website and see if it has any information about tickets."

Joyce seemed satisfied with that answer, because she nodded before returning her attention to the activities on the field. The skeleton of the pavilion had already been erected, and now a series of cranes were lifting the enormous canvas shell that would cover it. Off to one side were racks and racks of folding chairs, clearly waiting for the pavilion construction to be finished before they could be set in place.

For a few minutes, we were all quiet as we watched the huge tent take shape. I had to admit the whole operation was pretty impressive, including the way the workers moved briskly and efficiently, showing me that they'd done this plenty of times before. Around the perimeter of the work area, other little groups like ours watched as well, although they seemed to have turned the whole thing into something of a party, sipping coffee and eating cookies they'd obviously bought from Cloud Coffee, the coffee shop just down the street from my store.

Looking at them, I wished I'd thought of getting some refreshments. I generally didn't drink caffeine late in the day, but a nice hot chocolate with some whipped cream on top would've been the perfect thing on this cool, breezy fall day.

Just as I was about to suggest to Archie that we should head over to Cloud Coffee and get hot chocolate for everyone, a tall, slim woman with honey-blonde hair walked toward us. I'd never seen her before, but the clipboard she carried told me she must be someone who worked for Life Springs Church.

"Hello," she said pleasantly once she got close. She had a very faint Southern accent. Texas, maybe, or possibly someplace even deeper in that part of the country. "Enjoying the show?"

"It's very exciting," Joyce replied.

At once, the woman's bright blue eyes lit up. "Oh, are you a member of Pastor Galloway's congregation?"

Joyce's posture grew a little tense, and her friend said quickly, "Oh, we both go to the Methodist church here in Globe. But we wanted to take a peek at the tent going up."

The woman's smile didn't flicker even the

slightest bit. "Well, I have to admit it is kind of a spectacle. And even if you go to another church, all are welcome here. In fact, here are some passes that will get you in to hear Pastor Galloway's sermons."

She lifted the clip on her clipboard and extracted several pieces of cardstock, obviously the aforementioned passes. Joyce and Lynda looked thrilled to be given free entry to the event, but when the woman tried to hand one to Archie, he only lifted an eyebrow.

"No, thank you," he said. His tone was polite enough, but it seemed obvious to me that he would rather have been handed one of Sadie's full poopie bags. "I'm not much of a churchgoer."

Again, the woman's expression didn't waver even a little. "Oh, ours isn't your usual kind of church," she returned. "I think you'll find some of the sermons quite enlightening."

Once again, I found myself having to step in. "That's very kind of you…." I said, then trailed off, since she hadn't introduced herself.

Her smile widened. "Chelsea Haven," she supplied. "I'm Pastor Galloway's assistant."

The woman herself, the one who'd reached out to Calvin to see about getting some of his deputies to moonlight as security guards at the event. Well, I supposed it wasn't so surprising that she was here supervising the pavilion setup if she really was Pastor Galloway's right-hand woman. "Selena Marx," I said. "I run a shop downtown called Once in a Blue Moon."

For the first time, Chelsea Haven's studiously cheery expression slipped a little. From the flicker of suspicion I thought I glimpsed in her eyes, it seemed clear enough to me that she knew all about my store and what I sold…and didn't think much of it.

Well, Josie *had* warned me.

"My cousin Archie and I both follow a different path," I went on, figuring I'd already stuck my foot in it, so I might as well keep going. "But I hope you'll have a very successful event."

"Oh, it will be," Chelsea assured us, although I couldn't help noticing the way her attention was now fixed mainly on Joyce and Lynda, as if she'd already decided that Archie and I were lost causes.

Both of them suddenly lit up as though they'd just seen Brad Pitt walk by, and I raised an eyebrow, even as I shot a surreptitious glance over one shoulder to see what had piqued their interest.

A man was approaching our little group, someone I'd never seen before. But I somehow knew exactly who he must be.

As much as I could, I tried not to judge people purely by appearances. However, one look at Aaron Galloway told me he was pretty much exactly what I'd expected—expensive haircut, tan that had come either from a spray booth or the donations of his congregation so he could go on Caribbean vacations, brilliantly white teeth to complement his bronze complexion. His hair was brown and his eyes blue, and although he couldn't match Calvin's impressive six feet, five inches, the pastor was no slouch, probably at least an inch or two over six feet tall.

"Good afternoon, ladies," he said, pointedly ignoring Archie's presence in our little group. His voice was a practiced baritone, and, like Chelsea, he had a touch of a Southern accent. "Enjoying the show?"

"Oh, it's fascinating," Joyce replied, now sounding a little breathless. Clearly, she was thrilled to be in the pastor's exalted presence.

Too bad I couldn't say the same thing for myself. Archie now wore an expression so neutral that I could practically smell his disapproval from where I stood, and as for me…well, I couldn't help noticing the way Pastor Galloway's gaze moved from Joyce to Lynda almost dismissively before it landed on me. A gleam I didn't like at all entered those piercing blue eyes, and I found myself wishing I were anywhere but here.

"I'm glad you think so," he said, although he wasn't looking at Joyce as he spoke, but still stared at me.

I crossed my arms so the lovely diamond Calvin had given me and its accompanying band stood out clearly against my jacket. "We don't get spectacles like this in Globe very often," I commented.

Aaron Galloway's eyes might have narrowed just the slightest bit. "Oh, this is much more than a spectacle," he returned. "We're here to spread the word of the Lord."

And apparently ogle any halfway attractive women under forty who might be in the immediate vicinity. I wondered what Jesus might think about that sort of behavior.

I was spared from having to think of a suitable response by Joyce saying, "And we're ready to hear it, Pastor Galloway. Ms. Haven here was kind enough to give us some passes to the event."

"Very kind of her," the pastor said, although something in his tone told me he wasn't too thrilled about his right-hand woman handing out freebies.

Chelsea obviously picked up on his disapproval, because she said hastily, "Oh, I think I see the site foreman signaling us, Aaron. We'd better go see what he wants."

"Of course," Pastor Galloway replied, then nodded at the rest of us. "You all have a lovely rest of your afternoon."

The two of them walked away after that, with Chelsea clearly happy to put as much space between our little group and her pastor as possible. Next to me, Archie wore a wry expression that told me he hadn't missed a single nuance of our interactions and was amused by them... probably because Pastor Galloway's behavior had only reinforced everything he was already thinking about Life Springs Church and the people associated with it.

Luckily, Joyce and Lynda were so thrilled by the free passes Chelsea Haven had given them — and by getting to meet the man himself — that they didn't appear to have noticed anything off about our exchange. Instead, they were already plotting how to make the most of those unexpected freebies, although Lynda paused at the end of their little convo to add, "Selena, you should've taken the free ticket. It would be fun for all of us to go together and have lunch or something."

While the invitation warmed my heart, wild horses couldn't have dragged me to the Life Springs event. Maybe it might have been interesting from an anthropological standpoint—if nothing else—but I knew my presence at such a gathering would only lead to speculation among certain denizens of Globe that maybe I'd finally seen the light and had decided to leave my heathen ways behind.

Which was never going to happen. It might have surprised my detractors to learn that I considered myself highly spiritual, and certainly believed in a higher power at work in the universe. However, those beliefs didn't include the sort of all-seeing God that formed the center of their religions, which meant I definitely wasn't about to attend a televangelist's revival meeting any time in the near future…especially when the televangelist in question seemed like a world-class jerk.

"I have to be at the store," I said lightly, which was only the truth.

"Just on Saturday," Joyce pointed out. Since I sold her wonderful handmade candles in my shop and she came by frequently to replenish my stock, she had a very clear idea of Once in a Blue Moon's business hours. "You could still have come to the revival on Sunday."

"Calvin has the day off," I replied. "We already had plans to go to Gilbert to shop and have lunch."

Again, only the truth. He did his best to have

as many Sundays off as possible so we could spend some glorious free time together, but it didn't happen every weekend. As he'd told me on several occasions, it wouldn't be fair to his deputies for him to work a regular nine-to-five during the week and make them cover all the weekend shifts.

Joyce looked disappointed, but to my relief, she didn't try to argue with me. "Well, I suppose some of the services will end up online eventually," she said. "You could always watch them later."

Personally, I'd rather be tied to a stake and forced to watch Spongebob cartoons on repeat until my eyes bled, but I didn't voice that opinion out loud. No, I just offered her a little smile and said, "Maybe."

To my relief, Sadie started tugging at her leash right then, signaling that she was tired of standing there and listening to us chat, and wanted to be taken on a proper walk. I murmured a few words of apology to Joyce and Lynda, and headed across the grass, Archie at my side.

He waited until Sadie had anointed one of her favorite trees, and then said, "Should we have taken those passes? Ms. Haven didn't look very happy about us turning them down."

No, she hadn't. But I'd learned a long time

ago that it wasn't worth compromising my beliefs in a misguided attempt to keep the peace. I said as much to Archie, and he nodded, looking thoughtful.

"I suppose you're right," he replied, and I shot him a wry smile.

"What, you're actually agreeing with me about something?" I teased, but his expression remained solemn.

"Yes," he said calmly, "because what you're saying is simple common sense. Sometimes being polite can actually be detrimental. In this case, there was no point in giving Ms. Haven false hope, or making her or her pastor think they would ever have a chance of winning us over."

"Exactly," I said. "And besides, I definitely wouldn't want to take those passes and end up throwing them away when doing so might mean I was depriving someone else of a chance to go to an event they really wanted to attend."

"Very altruistic of you," Archie observed, now sounding a bit more like his usual ironic self.

"That's me," I replied. "Little miss sunshine and unicorns and rainbows."

He actually chuckled at that remark, as I'd hoped he would, and we finished our circuit of the park and headed back to the store. Because I planned to go straight home, we walked to the back of the building where my Jeep was parked, and we said goodbye before I loaded Sadie into the passenger seat and Archie unlocked the back door to the shop. He gave me a brief wave before going inside.

I returned the wave, then pulled out of my parking space and headed for home. Since Calvin was working late, I hadn't planned anything elaborate for dinner…which meant I had plenty of spare time on my hands.

And I knew exactly what I wanted to do with it.

Usually, performing a Tarot spread helped to relax me. I would hold a single question in my mind and open myself to the energies of the universe, then see what came of it.

In this particular case, though, I thought I probably should have left my Everyday Witch cards in their little velvet bag, poured myself a glass of wine, and called it a day.

Because when I'd pulled three cards to give me an indication of how the Life Springs Church visit in Globe was going to go, I'd pulled the Devil, the Tower, and my personal favorite, the Ten of Swords, the oh-so-lovely one with the poor witch lying face down on the ground with ten blades sticking out of her back.

Ouch.

It seemed the universe wasn't too pleased about the prospect of Pastor Galloway spreading his particular gospel in my adopted hometown.

As soon as the thought crossed my mind, I did my best to push it away. While this trio of cards looked calamitous on the surface, it didn't necessarily have anything to do with what Aaron Galloway preached in his sermons. I shouldn't be projecting my own biases on something that didn't directly affect me.

No, I needed to look at this logically.

The general meaning of the Devil card was of temptation, and also of clinging to attitudes or beliefs or behaviors that could be damaging to an individual. In this case, I honestly didn't know who might be holding on to elements in their life that might hurt them in the end. Pastor Galloway himself, or someone in his circle?

Maybe Chelsea Haven? I had to admit that on the surface, she certainly didn't look like someone who was wrestling with her inner demons. She was probably six or seven years older than I, and so in her late thirties, and had been dressed simply but attractively in a skirt suit and low-heeled shoes that wouldn't have slowed her down too much while performing her supervising duties at the park. Yes, I could tell she didn't much care for me or what I represented, but that didn't mean a whole heck of a lot. It's not as though it was the first time I'd encountered someone who inwardly thought I was going straight to hell.

And I also knew it wouldn't be the last.

I reminded myself that Aaron Galloway must have plenty of people working for him and that I shouldn't focus on Chelsea Haven just because she was the only one of them—besides the man himself, of course—that I'd met so far. Also, while the question had been centered on how the event would do, it didn't necessarily mean the universe was pointing me toward someone directly connected to Life Springs Church. Maybe this horrible outcome involved one of Globe's citizens instead.

That notion wasn't very appealing. Not that I was the type to wish ill on anyone, but if some calamity was going to befall an unsuspecting victim this weekend, I'd much rather it was a complete stranger rather than someone I knew and cared about.

The Tower seemed to indicate something was going to happen to shake up the status quo. Contrary to popular belief, it wasn't a completely negative card, as sometimes you needed your world to fall to ashes before you could begin to rebuild. Still, its presence in this reading told me something major was looming on the horizon, like monsoon clouds just beginning to build as the heat of the afternoon rose.

And as for the Ten of Swords, it also tended to signal that something less than desirable was bearing down on you with the speed of a freight train. In cases like that, about all you could do was brace for the worst…and know you still had the strength somewhere deep within to help you get back on your feet, brush yourself off, and keep moving forward.

Brace for the worst….

I stood there and stared down at the cards on the table in my office for a long moment. Usually, I loved this place, loved the way the afternoon sunlight slanted past the cottonwoods that lined a dry creek only yards away from the house, loved the feeling of peace I experienced whenever I entered the space. This room was bigger than the one I'd used for an office back at the apartment, and so Calvin had helped me set up more bookshelves on the wall opposite my altar and the shelving units that flanked it, bookshelves filled with crystals and plants and little trinkets and *objets d'art*…and books, of course, as many as I could fit amongst all the other items.

At the moment, though, I couldn't ignore the

unease churning in my stomach. I wished Calvin wasn't at work so I could talk over the spread with him and have him reassure me that it wasn't as bad as it looked. No, I wasn't afraid of being in the house alone, but I also couldn't ignore how big and empty it felt.

That glass of wine was sounding better and better.

I shuffled the cards back into the deck, slid it into its velvet pouch, and then returned the little bag to its usual resting spot on the bookshelf to my immediate right. As soon as I began to move, Sadie climbed out of her bed—we had dog beds scattered all over the house so she could be comfortable no matter what room we were in—and followed me to the kitchen. Once I got there, I pulled a half-drunk bottle of chardonnay from the fridge and poured myself a glass.

A couple of sips made me feel a little better, but I hadn't quite gotten rid of that sense of impending doom. And even though I tried to tell myself that while the cards didn't lie—though their interpretations were some- times hopelessly bungled by us clueless humans—it still didn't quite shake my feeling that something terrible was looming over all our heads.

Well, I wasn't completely helpless. If

nothing else, I could send Josie a warning that she should be on her guard.

Since I had no idea whether she might be with a client—she often had house showings at the end of the day, after prospective buyers were off work—I decided a text was my best course of action.

Hi, Josie, I wrote. *I just did a reading that has me a little concerned. I'm worried something might go down this weekend w/the Life Springs event. Just wanted to give you a heads-up so you could keep an eye out.*

And then I sent the message before I could lose my nerve and start telling myself I was blowing all this out of proportion.

She must have been at her office and not occupied with a client, because her reply came back almost immediately.

Thanks for the warning, she said, *but everything is on track and I can tell the people running the event are real professionals. I'm sure it will be fine.*

In other words, her reply was the written equivalent of one of her airy hand waves, the gesture she made whenever she wanted to dismiss something that wasn't part of her world view.

I wanted to be annoyed but couldn't quite allow myself. Josie had turned out to be one of my best friends—an improbable one, maybe, and yet a loyal friend nonetheless—except she had a stubborn blind spot when it came to my psychic gifts and the way I communicated with the energies of the universe. She wouldn't flat out deny I had abilities that most people didn't, but at the same time, she became extremely uncomfortable whenever I mentioned them.

Most of the time, this wasn't an issue. Our everyday lives hummed along just fine without me mentioning what I'd seen in my latest card spread, or what I might have discussed in my latest conversation with Grandma Ellen in my crystal ball.

Not that I'd had much reason to consult my grandmother lately. Life in Globe had been utter serenity these past six months, and my usual practice was to avoid bothering Grandma Ellen unless I had no other choice, since she'd made it clear she didn't appreciate me continually interrupting her in the afterlife over problems I could have figured out on my own.

I could have tried forcing the issue of my latest Tarot reading with Josie, but I decided against it. My friend had a tendency to dig in her heels whenever you pushed her too hard, and honestly, right now all I had was a somewhat disastrous Tarot reading to go on.

So I just wrote back, *Glad to hear it. I hope it all goes well.*

As I set down my phone, though, I knew this wouldn't be the end of it. Josie might think everything was just fine, and yet...

...and yet I knew I planned to keep my eyes open. Because if my past year and a half in Globe had taught me anything, it was that the universe had a way of broadsiding you when you least expected it.

4

Rubber Checks

ALTHOUGH I HAD ABSOLUTELY NO INTENTION OF attending any of the Life Springs Church's events that weekend, that still didn't mean I couldn't do a little research, just to let myself know what Globe was getting itself into. The church had a YouTube channel where it looked as though they'd archived all of Pastor Galloway's sermons from the past five years or more…all of the listings with helpful links at the end where you could go onto the church's website and make an online contribution.

Fat chance, I thought wryly. While I had made some hefty charitable donations since becoming a millionaire thanks to my inheritance from Lucien Dumond—including quite a few sizable gifts to Josie's beloved Old Globe Theatre Company—I definitely had no intention of giving anything to Life Springs Church. To be quite honest, any church that took in way more than it needed for operating expenses and bought its pastors private jets or multimillion-dollar mansions definitely didn't need my money.

Not that I was certain Life Springs fell into that category, but it sure seemed to me as if they had plenty of money to throw around, judging by the elaborate setup of their event here in Globe.

I chose one of the more recent sermons and hit "play" on the remote for our Apple TV. After fast-forwarding through a couple of hymns and a little speech from a woman who appeared to be introducing Pastor Galloway, he walked up to the pulpit.

On screen, he looked taller than in real life —a trick of the camera angle, I was sure. His blue eyes shone, and his Southern-tinged baritone sounded extra resonant, again through some sort of special sound mixing...or maybe because he knew he was on stage and had to make the most of it. The sermon he delivered seemed to be about helping one's neighbor, but I didn't know whether his final summation included the church itself as one of those neighbors, since I switched the TV off after about five minutes.

By then, I had enough additional information to solidify my opinion of him. From what I'd seen so far, Aaron Galloway seemed to be cut from the same cloth—no pun intended—as just about every TV preacher I'd ever seen. Slickly attractive, persuasively voiced, and extremely skilled at making sure his ministry provided him with all of life's creature comforts.

Maybe I was being excessively judge-y, thanks to my one personal interaction with him, but I didn't think so. There was a certain type who tended to excel at his chosen line of work, and he appeared to fit that mold to a T.

Which meant absolutely nothing in the grand scheme of things. Just because every instinct I possessed told me the guy was slimy, that didn't signify he had any real connection to the Tarot reading I'd just performed. True, some might have argued—pretty convincingly—that anyone dedicated to separating his parishioners from their hard-earned money could very well be the real-life analogue of the Devil card I'd pulled, and yet for some reason, I didn't think the answer was quite that simple.

Or I could be making a mountain out of a molehill. It wasn't as though I hadn't performed readings in the past that promised all sorts of calamitous outcomes and then turned out to be nothing. It didn't happen all that often, because I prided myself on the accuracy of my readings, but no one…not even me…batted a thousand all the time.

With a sigh, I set down the remote and headed into the kitchen, figuring it was time to fix my long-delayed bowl of soup. Sadie, who'd been sitting by patiently as I watched Aaron Galloway's sermon, immediately got up from her bed in the living room and hurried after me. Yes, I'd fed her almost as soon as I walked in the door, but she lived in the hope that I might give her some choice morsels during dinner prep.

No such luck tonight, although I patted her head and gave her an extra treat while murmuring an apology about the pickings being pretty slim for this evening's meal. The clock on the microwave told me it was not quite seven-thirty, and I held back another sigh. While I understood why Calvin had to work late some nights, that didn't mean I had to be happy about it.

But I had my soup and made myself watch some completely mundane TV, Sadie curled in my lap. As soon as the front door opened at about a quarter after nine, however, she immediately bolted for the entryway, tail wagging furiously.

I might have been the one who found her, but that little dog absolutely adored Calvin.

He bent down to pet her head while she stood on her hind legs and danced around, tail still going a hundred miles an hour. Not for the first time, I found myself smiling at the contrast between my husband, who stood almost six foot five in his sock feet, and the little chi mix who occupied such a large space in my heart and who weighed maybe ten pounds soaking wet.

"Hey, there," I called to him from the living room, and he came in to see me, Sadie bobbing and weaving around him. How neither of us had managed to trip over her and break multiple necks in the process, I honestly had no idea.

"Hey," Calvin said, then settled himself on the couch next to me. At once, the dog jumped up and pushed her paws against his chest, trying to get a few licks in on his cheeks and chin. "Looks like someone missed me."

"We both did," I replied.

He paused and took a good look at my face. "Everything okay, Selena?"

"Oh, sure," I said at once, even though I really wasn't certain whether that was the truth. "I guess I'm just having a case of the heebie-jeebies."

"Any particular reason why, or is this only a case of overwhelming existential dread?"

Judging by the faint glint in his dark eyes as he asked me that question, I guessed he was at least partly joking. We'd been together long enough that he knew I wasn't the sort to get angsty for no reason, mostly because I'd realized long ago that the universe had our best interests at heart, even if the route it had us travel sometimes didn't make much sense.

I explained the Tarot reading I'd done a few hours earlier, then concluded with, "It's entirely possible I'm making mountains out of molehills, but my intuition says no, that something's going to happen. I just don't know what. I did my best to warn Josie, except she obviously didn't want to hear it."

"Well, I can see why," Calvin replied, his tone now thoughtful. "She's got a lot riding on this Life Springs event, since it sounds like they're paying the town a pretty big chunk of cash for the privilege of holding their event here. Or at least, that's my best guess after hearing the hourly rate they're paying my deputies for working security."

"Deep pockets?" I asked, although I'd already surmised that Pastor Galloway's church had plenty of money to throw around.

"Sure seems like it," Calvin said, "considering they're paying almost double what my guys earn on their regular paychecks."

Wow. True, it wasn't as though the Life Springs' compensation was a regular salary, only what they were paying for a limited number of hours over the weekend, but still.

And obviously, I hadn't asked Josie what the city was earning for hosting the event here, but it was pretty easy to guess that it had to be a considerable amount. No wonder she hadn't wanted to listen to my Cassandra-like prophecies of doom.

Okay, not utter doom…most likely…but still, something that might throw a monkey wrench into the whole carefully planned enterprise.

"But I'll tell my guys to keep an eye out," he continued. "I mean, that's what they're getting paid to do, but still, if they hear it from me, too, then they'll probably take it more seriously."

I reached over and squeezed his hand. "Thanks, hon," I said. "I don't know what I'd do without you."

"Oh, probably get scooped up by the next millionaire sorcerer who came along," Calvin said with a grin, and I felt compelled to give him a light smack on the arm.

"I'd rather be single for the rest of my life," I declared, and he bent over and gave me a quick kiss.

"Luckily, I don't think you'll need to worry about that."

Another kiss, deeper, more passionate this time, and then he took my hand in his and led me to the bedroom.

I was all too happy to go. Spending this time with Calvin was the perfect way to take my mind off Life Springs Church…and what its presence in Globe actually meant.

The next morning was eerily quiet for a Saturday. Not that I'd really been expecting a lot of Pastor Galloway's flock to pop in to pick up a deck of Tarot cards or a hunk of rose quartz to put under their pillows to combat insomnia and block nightmares, but I hadn't thought quite so many of the locals would give up their regular weekend routines to attend the tent revival.

Then again, there wasn't a whole heck of a lot going on in our neck of the woods. I found it entirely plausible that quite a few people had decided to go to the event out of curiosity and not much else. Bucking national trends, a majority of Globe's citizens actually did attend church on a regular basis, but since they'd already picked their teams, so to speak, I couldn't think of any other reasons except boredom and general nosiness for them to check out the goings-on in the big tent less than a quarter-mile away from my shop.

A few of my regulars did drift in and out that morning, so it wasn't completely dead at the store. And then a little after one, right after I'd finished my lunch break—I'd given Archie the day off, since I knew Victoria was coming out to see him this weekend—Josie walked into the store, stopped dead next to the little table that held this month's display of thematic crystals and books, and announced dramatically, "I knew I should have listened to you!"

I blinked at her. "Excuse me?"

"About Life Springs Church," she returned, now sounding irritated, as if I should have known right away what she was referring to. "Their check *bounced!*"

Once again, I couldn't do much more than blink. "They didn't pay by cashier's check?"

Now Josie hesitated for a second or two, as though she realized she'd made a misstep and, as the town's newest mayor, didn't want to admit to such an obvious mistake. But after that brief falter, her righteous indignation picked up steam again as she said, "Well, I told Chelsea Haven that wasn't necessary, since they were having to do everything so last minute. And then I got an alert from the bank this morning that their check was returned for insufficient funds."

Yikes. Was this the calamity the Tarot cards had been warning me about? At first glance, it certainly seemed sufficient to cause quite a bit of havoc—our little town needed that money, especially since it would be Globe's services that covered picking up the trash at the site of the revival, as well as the beefed-up police presence such a sizable crowd demanded, even if the church was paying for Calvin's deputies to moonlight as their private security force.

Which immediately made me wonder if the deputies were going to get stiffed, too. Maybe the church had offered such extravagant sums to pay them for their services because Chelsea Haven or whoever was holding the purse strings had absolutely no intention of making good on the deal.

As soon as that thought crossed my mind, though, I immediately dismissed it. If nothing else, leaving a bunch of Native American cops in the lurch would be very bad optics. "I'm sure it has to be some kind of a mistake," I said slowly, hoping Josie wouldn't jump down my throat for even that limp defense of the church.

Her eyes narrowed, but it seemed I must have been on the right track, because she gave a grudging nod. "I called Chelsea Haven immediately, of course, and she apologized profusely. She told me that she'd been hurrying and accidentally wrote the check from a different account than the one they used for large expenditures, and that she'd have a cashier's check for me first thing Monday morning."

"Well, then," I said, thinking it seemed as though Josie was making a big production out of what appeared to be an honest mistake, "it sounds like you've already got it sorted out."

"Maybe," she said grudgingly. "But I know I won't rest easy until I have that cashier's check in hand. The Life Springs people will be packing up on Monday, so I assume Ms. Haven will take care of it sometime that morning, but...."

The words trailed off, but I guessed what was probably running through my friend's thoughts right then. Yes, Pastor Galloway's right-hand woman had promised to make good on their debts, but Josie was probably envisioning them all slipping off under cover of darkness sometime in the wee hours of Monday morning and leaving Globe's unfortunate mayor holding the proverbial bag.

"I really think it will be fine," I assured her. Figuring that my somewhat jaded thoughts of a moment earlier might serve to allay Josie's fears, I added, "After all, it would look pretty bad to have a mega-church stiff some poor little town in the middle of nowhere out of the fees they'd been promised."

At once, Josie drew herself up. "We are not a 'poor little town in the middle of nowhere.'"

About all I could do was smile. "Well, you know that and I know that," I said. "But we also both know that if the Phoenix TV stations—or especially the national news—pick up the story, that's pretty much exactly how they're going to frame it. Anyway, this just sounds like a hiccup to me."

My friend didn't respond immediately, most likely because she was turning over my words in her mind and trying to decide whether she agreed with them or not. After a moment, she said grudgingly, "I suppose so. And Ms. Haven really did sound upset about what happened. Why, she even invited me to be backstage at Pastor Galloway's sermon tomorrow morning!"

I wasn't sure whether I'd really regard such an invitation as an honor, but Josie seemed excited by it, which meant I needed to keep my mouth shut. "That sounds like fun," I replied in the most neutral tones possible.

Immediately, her light blue eyes brightened. "You should come with me!" she exclaimed.

"Oh, no," I demurred, thanking the Goddess that I had a ready excuse I could hand my friend. "I mean, I already have some plans with Calvin, and we've got a ton of stuff we need to do around the house. Remember, we're hosting Thanksgiving dinner for twelve on Thursday."

Josie's expression deflated a little. "Oh, of course," she said. "I'd forgotten about that. I suppose it must be a little nerve-wracking to have to prep a meal for so many people."

It wasn't the cooking I was worried about—Calvin and I already planned to smoke two medium-sized turkeys in the enormous, commercial-grade smoker he'd bought earlier this fall, and I loved to cook, so putting together all the various side dishes to go with the turkey wasn't too daunting a prospect.

No, it was making sure the house was absolutely perfect and up to Delia Standingbear's exacting standards. It wasn't that I was a slob—my moon in Virgo ensured my house was pretty much always tidy—but more that I wanted to make sure my new mother-in-law couldn't find fault with a single thing. Before Calvin and I got married, it had been her duty to cook big holiday meals for as much of the Standingbear clan as would fit in their sprawling pueblo-style home, and it had taken some convincing for her to allow me to host this year's Thanksgiving dinner. I needed to make sure I didn't let her—or Calvin—down.

"Oh, I think it will be fine," I told Josie. "But because I'm working all week at the shop, I need to get as much done tomorrow as I can."

She gave a resigned nod. All of her major holidays were spent with her nephew Brett and his wife Terry and their three small children, as Josie was divorced and never had any kids of her own, and that was why she wouldn't be attending Calvin's and my Thanksgiving feast. I would have loved to have her there, but the only way she wouldn't spend time with her own family during a holiday was if they were traveling. Since Brett and his wife rarely left Globe—their recent trip to Hawaii for their anniversary notwithstanding—I kind of doubted that was going to happen.

"But I'll expect you to give me a full report on Monday morning," I added, and immediately Josie's expression brightened. "Maybe we can run out for coffee while Archie holds down the fort."

"That sounds like a good idea," she said. "Assuming I've gotten this mess with the Life Springs payment handled by then."

"Well, lunch at Olamendi's, then," I replied. "Whichever works."

"I'll plan on it." Her phone rang then, and she pulled it out of the oversized rust-colored leather purse she had slung over one shoulder. I still hadn't been able to get an accurate count of Josie's bags—it seemed as though she had a different one for almost every outfit—but I thought she must have at least two dozen, if not more. A glance at the screen, and she held the phone to her ear while shooting me an apologetic glance. "Hi, Lauren. Yes, we're still on for two. I'll see you then." A small gust of an exasperated breath as she returned the phone to an inner pocket of her purse, and then she said, "I swear, that woman acts as though buying a house is like giving birth. She needs her hand held every step of the way."

I gave a sympathetic nod. Because Josie had helped me buy the building that housed the apartment and the store, I knew she tended to go above and beyond, and seemed to be on call twenty-four hours a day, every day of the week. Most of her clients didn't take advantage of her willingness to do whatever it took to make sure a sale went smoothly, but every once in a while, she got a real doozy. I didn't know who "Lauren" was—during my time in Globe, I'd gotten to know a lot of people but definitely didn't have every citizen of my adopted hometown memorized—but it sounded as though she was one of those uncomfortable exceptions.

"Then I won't keep you," I said. "Good luck with your client."

"I'll need it," she replied, still sounding exasperated. "And I'll pop in when I can on Monday to give you a full report on everything that happens at the Life Springs event tomorrow morning."

While I could have lived without such a recitation, I managed to assume what I hoped was an appropriately enthusiastic smile and said, "Looking forward to it."

She responded with a smile of her own and then headed out. I watched her go, my own smile slipping as soon as the front door to the shop closed behind her.

Why couldn't I shake the feeling that this mess with the payment from Life Springs Church wasn't the disaster the cards had foretold, and that something much worse lurked on the horizon?

5

Half Caf With a Twist

BUT THE REST OF THE DAY WAS JUST AS QUIET as the morning had been, and I closed up promptly at five and headed for home. It still felt just the slightest bit strange to get in my Jeep and drive away rather than walk up the steps to the apartment over the shop, but enough months had passed by now that it was a momentary twinge and nothing more.

Besides, I'd spotted Victoria's red Mercedes GLA parked next to Archie's hand-me-down Beetle, and so I knew they were both in the apartment at the moment.

Doing what, I probably didn't want to speculate.

Calvin hadn't worked that day, and so he was hanging out in the living room watching TV, Sadie curled up in his lap. To my infinite relief, he had absolutely no interest in football, and so he was currently viewing some kind of cooking video on YouTube, one where a balding man with an oversized mustache was smoking a turkey in the same oversized unit we'd bought a few months prior.

"Doing research, I see," I said after I'd bent down to give Calvin a kiss—and dodging Sadie's overtures, since it was clear she wanted to bestow a few slobbery kisses of her own.

"I figured I might as well see what some of the experts had to say," he replied as he paused the video. "We definitely made the right choice in smoking two birds instead of one—with the really big ones, it's not safe to have them cooking at low temperatures for that many hours —but I'm waiting for him to move on to smoking more than one at a time."

"You could just fast-forward the video, you know," I said, and Calvin shrugged.

"Maybe, but then I might miss some important tidbit."

That was my husband all over again. He'd always been the methodical type, someone who wanted to make sure no angles had been overlooked, no "i"s undotted and "t"s uncrossed. Those qualities made him an excellent police chief, but every once in a while, they also made me—who tended to be a lot more impulsive — just the teeniest bit impatient.

Deciding I might as well let it go, I instead responded, "Hey, have any of your deputies mentioned that they had a problem getting paid by the Life Springs people?"

At once, his brows drew together. "No," he said. "But I'm pretty sure they aren't going to get their checks until the event is over. Why?"

Briefly, I explained about how Josie's check from Chelsea Haven had bounced. "I know it was probably just a mix-up," I finished. "But it still might not hurt to give them a heads-up, just in case."

Calvin's frown remained in place. "I'm not sure about that," he said slowly. "Even if this really was just an honest mistake, then that might make them less inclined to show up for work tomorrow."

I hadn't thought of that angle, but I realized he was right. Anyway, I'd already quietly resolved to myself that if the Life Springs Church crew really did end up bilking Globe out of all those fees, then I'd pay their debt myself. If Josie wanted to take them to court to recover the lost funds, that would be her decision, but at least the town wouldn't be hurting either way. And I would certainly pay the deputies what they'd earned. It wasn't as though doing so would make a noticeable dent in any of my numerous accounts, since it seemed as though no matter how much money I donated, the capital just kept growing. I supposed that was the nice thing about compound interest.

"Okay," I said. "It was just a thought."

"And one motivated by worry for them, so I appreciate it," Calvin replied. "But there's no point in putting them on edge for no reason."

I nodded. "I understand. What's for dinner?"

He might have grimaced very slightly at the abrupt change in topic. However, he answered right away, saying, "Oh, I've got beef stew in the crockpot. But if you could make some biscuits to go with it…."

"Consider it done," I said with a grin. Over the past few months, he'd been doing his best to put dinner together on those days when I worked and he didn't, even though he wasn't exactly what you could call hugely experienced in the kitchen. But he'd built up a little repertoire of dishes he could manage, and continued to add new recipes here and there. His beef stew was actually delicious, although he hadn't yet mastered the art of baking from scratch.

Whereas I loved to bake, and knew I could whip up a batch of fluffy biscuits without batting an eye.

"You are definitely a woman after my own

heart," he said, and I gave him another kiss, this one a healthy smack on the lips.

"And the rest of you as well," I returned. "But we can discuss that later."

He slanted a look up at me that promised all sorts of fun in the very near future.

Now, however, I had some biscuits to make.

Even though Calvin and I had planned to go to Gilbert for lunch, after looking over our lengthy to-do list, we decided that Sunday needed to be all about work and no play. Calvin miraculously had the whole weekend off, and so he dutifully scrubbed bathrooms and floors while I dusted and made sure the kitchen was absolutely immaculate. Some people might have argued there wasn't much point in doing a deep clean with days to go until Thanksgiving arrived, but I knew I simply wouldn't have time during the week. We'd just need to be careful not to make a mess between now and then, and on the day of the big dinner, I'd dust the furniture in the main rooms of the house all over again, and wipe down the guest bathroom as well.

It actually felt good to do all that work, to really get into the corners and make sure any dust bunnies that had decided to take up residence there since the last time we'd cleaned like this had been banished from existence. True, I probably could have hired Lupe Olvera, the housekeeper my mother employed to keep her and Tom's big Victorian mansion in tiptop shape, to do the cleaning for me, but I liked that Calvin and I were working together to make sure our home was ready for all our guests. Whether I'd still feel the same way a year from now, I didn't know, but I told myself I could figure that out when the time came.

Once we were done with the cleaning, we sat down for an afternoon snack of some cheese and a glass of wine. We'd already promised one another dinner at the restaurant in the Gold Dust Casino so we wouldn't mess up the kitchen right after we'd cleaned it, but our reservations were for seven o'clock and we were both hungry after the day's exertions.

However, I'd only had a few sips of wine and a couple of bites of cheese—bites I shared with Sadie, so they weren't all that big—before my cell phone rang.

"Just ignore it," Calvin said, then took a swallow of rosé. "It's Sunday afternoon. How important could it be?"

A large part of me wanted to agree with him. We'd just sat down, and my back was aching from all that kitchen scrubbing. I could check the message after we were done with our midday snack and handle it then.

Something in my bones was telling me I needed to answer this particular call, though. And when my intuition prodded at me like that, I knew better than to ignore it.

"No, I'd better pick up," I told him as I wearily rose from the couch. "Maybe Archie's having car trouble or something. He mentioned to me the other day that he and Victoria were thinking of going up to Payson."

Calvin lifted an eyebrow but didn't say anything. He knew as well as I did that, although I'd given Archie my Volkswagen because he needed wheels and I had my new Jeep, the couple tended to drive Victoria's little Mercedes SUV, probably because it was much newer and had a lot more creature comforts. Her vehicle was only a little more than a year old, which meant it was certainly covered under its manufacturer's fancy roadside assistance program.

I'd left the phone sitting on a side table where I kept one of its chargers. The number on the screen was Josie's, and for some reason, a chill worked its way down my spine.

"Hello?" I said, hoping I was having a heebie-jeebie flash for no reason. "This is Selena."

"Thank God you're home," came Josie's voice. "Something terrible has happened."

The two of us sat at the table in Josie's kitchen, drinking a pot of English Breakfast tea she'd insisted on brewing herself. Her hands looked a little shaky after her ordeal, but because it was Josie Woodward, I could tell she wanted to pretend everything was fine.

Unfortunately, it most decidedly wasn't.

"Tell me what happened," I said. She'd given me a jumbled story about Pastor Galloway collapsing backstage at the Life Springs event just before he was due to go onstage and deliver his Sunday morning sermon and how he was then rushed off to the hospital, but I still wasn't entirely clear about the sequence of events.

Josie reached up to pat a nonexistent hair back in place. "Well, I was backstage at the revival, like I said," she replied. At least she sounded a little steadier now than she had on the phone, even if she still looked pretty rattled. "It was definitely more chaotic than I'd thought it would be, with people rushing around and checking on the sound equipment and the lighting, that kind of thing. Pastor Galloway was off to one side getting a makeup touch-up, and was angry because his coffee had gone missing. Chelsea Haven said she knew the order had been delivered by Cloud Coffee and asked me if I minded going to look for it, since everyone else was busy. Of course, I told her that would be no problem, and so I poked around a little bit and found one of those cardboard carriers sitting on a table that had some gadgets and electrical cords piled on it. The carrier had two cups of coffee, one with Pastor Galloway's name written on it, so I picked it up and took it over to him. He thanked me and drank about half his coffee, I think, and then went over to talk to Ms. Haven about something."

A pause while Josie drank some tea, then set the cup back in its saucer with a faint rattle. I waited, knowing I shouldn't push her, should let her tell her story as she saw fit.

"But then…." She pulled in a breath. The blush she wore stood out starkly against her white cheeks; I didn't think I'd ever seen her look so pale. "But then Pastor Galloway clutched his stomach as if he was having a cramp or something, and doubled over. I heard Chelsea asking him if he was all right, and he just shook his head at her and then collapsed onto the floor. She called 9-1-1, and an ambulance came and took him away about five minutes later. He was writhing in pain by that time, moaning about his stomach. Chelsea had to go on stage after the ambulance was gone and tell everyone that the pastor had been taken suddenly ill and that the day's events were canceled. She left as soon as she made her little speech so she could go to the hospital." Josie's worried blue eyes, almost the color of a baby blanket I'd had when I was just a toddler, met mine. "It's what you saw in the cards, isn't it? Something terrible really did happen at the Life Springs Church event."

Sometimes, I really hated it when the Tarot was so on the nose. Still, I wasn't quite ready to jump to conclusions. "It does sound pretty awful," I said gently. "But it also sounds like the EMTs got there right away. If Pastor Galloway was having a heart attack, then a quick response like that probably saved him."

My friend didn't look as relieved by my words as I'd hoped she would. "But he was clutching his stomach," she pointed out. "Not his chest."

"I know," I replied. "But severe stomach pains can be another warning sign of a heart attack. Or maybe he has ulcers or something, and they flared up. Either way, the hospital will be able to figure it out."

For the first time, some of the worry that had

tightened Josie's features seemed to lessen a bit. "You really think so?"

"I'm sure of it," I said. And I wasn't just blowing smoke—the small regional hospital located on the east end of town might have been dwarfed by its urban analogues, but the doctors and nurses there were top-notch. Whatever was wrong with Aaron Galloway, I had no doubt they'd figure it out…and quickly.

We drank tea in silence for a moment or two. I could tell Josie was still trying to process what had happened, trying to reassure herself that even if my Tarot cards might have predicted something like this would happen, the worst was now over and Pastor Galloway could get the treatment he needed. It might not have been anything close to what he'd had planned for this particular Sunday sermon, but he'd be fine in the end.

Something else occurred to me. "Or it could have been a panic attack," I said. "I think I read somewhere that sometimes those can make you feel like you're having a heart attack."

Josie looked immediately skeptical at that suggestion, one auburn-penciled brow lifting slightly. "Why would the pastor have a panic attack? Yes, I know lots of people are frightened of speaking in public, but that's what he does for a living, isn't it?"

Her answer made me feel a little foolish. She was right, after all—we weren't talking about some scared high school kid getting up to make a speech about how they should be elected class treasurer, but a man who apparently had spent most of his adult life talking in front of crowds. A panic attack seemed highly unlikely.

At the same time, though, I didn't see any reason to take that particular theory off the table. Sometimes our bodies reacted to stimuli in ways we couldn't anticipate.

I shrugged and sipped some of my own tea, then said, "Yes, but it's still possible. About all any of us can do is wait to see what the hospital has to say."

"If they say anything at all," Josie replied darkly, mouth with its coating of coral lipstick pursing. "It's not as though Pastor Galloway is related to any of us. There's no reason for them to keep us updated."

"Oh, I think they will," I told her. "Aaron Galloway is a public figure, and his visit here was well-publicized. I think the hospital will have to hold some kind of press conference just to let everyone know what happened and what his prognosis is."

Her fingers—tipped with a deep russet nail polish that matched the purse she'd been carrying the day before—tapped against the side of her cup. "I suppose you're right," she said after a brief pause. "And I have to say it was a good thing that Calvin loaned those deputies of his to Life Springs Church for the weekend, because they were definitely needed to help disperse the crowd after it was clear there weren't going to be any sermons today."

I almost told her Calvin hadn't exactly "loaned" them, that they were getting paid well for their presence there, but I figured it wasn't worth getting quite so nitpicky. However, Josie's comment provided further cause for concern. After all, if the church really ended up bilking the town of Globe out of all those fees, I could only imagine they probably wouldn't be too concerned about leaving the San Ramon Apache deputies hanging as well.

Not for the first time, I told myself not to borrow trouble. Chelsea Haven had assured Josie the fees would be paid. True, she and the rest of the people who worked for Life Springs Church had just been thrown a serious curveball, but I had to hope that whatever was ailing Pastor Galloway, it was something he'd recover from quickly and so could be back on the prose-lytizing trail soon enough. It might not help the people here in town who'd missed out on the second day of the event, and yet this sort of thing happened all the time. In the end, this small mishap would only be a blip on the town's radar.

"I'm sure people were disappointed there wasn't a sermon from the pastor today," I said, thinking it was probably better to focus on the reactions from the crowd rather than the problematic subject of the church's non-payment.

"Oh, they were," Josie said. "I wasn't down in the crowd with everyone, of course, but I heard some grumbling. Still, the deputies made sure everyone moved along without too much trouble. By the time I left, the park was pretty much empty. Ms. Haven was gone, of course, but there were a few people from the church who stayed behind to put away the sound equipment and pack up the chairs. I assume they'll leave the tent in place, since the company that set it up is supposed to come back tomorrow to take it down."

Once upon a time, I might have wondered how Josie had found out about all this. However, it hadn't taken me long to figure out that she seemed to know everything there was to know about her beloved town, even if the precise means of her collecting all that data still wasn't completely clear to me. Besides, she had been well-connected enough when she was only the town's premiere real estate agent, but now that she was mayor as well, I had to believe she had acquired even more means of gathering information.

At any rate, it sounded to me as though the practical side of things was being handled well enough. About all anyone could do at this point was wait to see how things went with Aaron Galloway.

"Well, it's definitely unfortunate," I said after having another sip of tea.

Josie made a sound of agreement, although her expression was still troubled. I could tell she wasn't happy about the way the entire situation had been left hanging, but at least it sounded to me as though the Life Springs people had enough of a support network in place that Globe wouldn't be stuck with having to remove the pavilion or any other equipment they might have brought with them.

The doorbell rang, and Josie lifted a puzzled eyebrow. "That's strange," she said. "I wasn't expecting any company."

Maybe not, but I knew her neighbors tended to drop by if they wanted to gossip—and the Goddess only knows they all had plenty to gossip about right now.

"Well, better see who it is," I told her. "In case it's something important."

She nodded and excused herself, and left the kitchen so she could head down the hall to the front door. Because it was nearly a straight shot from where we'd been sitting to the entryway, I could still hear her clearly enough.

"Henry?" she said, sounding startled.

At once, I froze. If Henry Lewis—the only Henry I knew in Globe—was at Josie's front door on a Sunday afternoon, it couldn't mean anything good.

"Sorry, Josie," Chief Lewis said. "I'm afraid I have to arrest you for the murder of Aaron Galloway."

6

Improbable Cause

THIS WHOLE SITUATION HAD A FEELING OF nightmarish déjà vu—sitting in the waiting area at the police station, breathing in air that always seemed to smell of stale coffee and, very faintly, of feet.

The main difference was that this time, I had Calvin sitting next to me rather than him being locked up in a cell and waiting for me to bail him out. As soon as Henry took Josie away, I called my husband and told him he needed to meet me at the station, stat.

Of course, all our hurry was for nothing, because as soon as we got there, we were informed by the worried-looking deputy at the front desk—Loretta Stillman, who usually sat there, wasn't working that day—that they were still booking Josie Woodrow and that we'd have to wait to hear from the judge regarding her bail.

In a way, getting that piece of information made me feel a little bit better. It meant Henry Lewis regarded the case seriously enough that he'd rousted the D.A. on a Sunday afternoon to have her formally arraigned. Some people might not have viewed those actions as particularly heartening, but at least it meant we'd be able to post bail for Josie once the amount had been set, and that she wouldn't have to wait until Monday morning and therefore spend the night in jail.

"How is this even possible?" Calvin asked. He still looked pretty gobsmacked, and I couldn't really blame him for that. "Wasn't Aaron Galloway alive when last seen?"

"He must have passed away after the EMTS took him to the hospital," I replied. "I don't know what happened. All I know is that there's no way in the world Josie could be responsible for the man's death. The whole thing is crazy."

"Well, there had to be some kind of physical evidence," Calvin said. "Otherwise, I don't see how Henry would have arrested someone who's a friend…and the town's mayor."

I shook my head. "I guess so," I said. "On the other hand, we both know the chief is kind of trigger-happy when it comes to this kind of thing."

About all Calvin could do was grimace slightly. Although the charges against him had been dropped and it had been proven beyond a shadow of a doubt that Thad Sullivan, Dillon James' manager and co-producer, was the man who'd killed him, I could tell my husband was less than thrilled to be back in the station where he'd spent an uncomfortable couple of hours before I bailed him out.

And, just like before, I had my checkbook with me, because Gila County didn't believe in electronic payments for the important stuff.

I was getting Josie out of here just as soon as I could...no matter what.

Before Calvin could say anything, Josie's nephew Brett came hurrying in, expression far wilder than I'd ever seen it before. In most cases, Brett was one of those men who never seemed to get too upset by anything. Now, though—now he looked downright panicked, face pale and his mouth tight.

As soon as he caught sight of Calvin and me, though, he seemed to calm down a bit, some of the strain slipping away from his pleasant, somewhat pointed features.

"Is she okay?" he asked. "She called me as soon as they'd let her, and I came over right away, but—"

"We don't know much yet," I said. "I was

with your aunt when Henry came to arrest her, and that's when I called Calvin and we came over to wait. It does sound as though she's getting arraigned today, though, so as soon as we know what her bail is, I'll post it and we'll get her out of here."

At once, Brett's light brown brows drew together. "I can't let you do that—"

"Oh, yes, you can," I cut in. Brett was very close to Josie and sort of looked on her as a second mother, but even though he was Globe's most skilled and successful handyman, it wasn't as though he had the kind of cash lying around to post his aunt's bail. Not with three kids and the second mortgage he and his wife had taken out to expand their modest three-bedroom house so everyone could have their own room, along with another bathroom and an updated kitchen. "Josie's one of my best friends, and I have the money to do it. So, just sit down and wait with us."

His mouth opened again, as though he wanted to argue further, but a very small head shake from Calvin signaled that additional protests wouldn't get him very far. Instead, Brett sat down on the empty chair to my left and let out a sigh.

"This is crazy," he said, and I gave a sympathetic nod.

"I know," I told him. "But we'll get this straightened out. If necessary, we'll help her hire the very best criminal defense attorney there is."

That offer didn't seem to reassure Brett. Once again he frowned, and panic flared in his hazel eyes. "You really think it'll get to that point?"

"I doubt it," Calvin put in. "What can seem like pretty solid grounds for arresting a person often gets shot down once more evidence is gathered. We just have to wait and see exactly why Henry Lewis thought your aunt had anything to do with Aaron Galloway's death."

"She couldn't have," Brett said. "My aunt wouldn't hurt a fly."

Well, that might have been stretching things a bit, since I'd personally seen her swat a spider or two when it was getting a little too close for comfort. All the same, sending a spider on to its next life wasn't quite the same as cold-bloodedly murdering a man.

"I know," I replied, my tone as soothing as I could make it. "And we'll get all this straightened out soon enough."

Brett sat up a little straighter on his metal and plastic chair, which I knew was just as uncomfortable as it looked, since I was sitting on its identical twin. "You'll have to solve the murder, Selena," he said. "Just like you did for Calvin. If you find the real murderer, then they'll have to drop all the charges against my aunt, right?"

Next to me, Calvin shifted on his chair and sent me a sideways warning glance, as if trying to tell me I needed to stay out of this. While my relationship with Henry had improved of late — probably because there hadn't been any murder cases for me to interfere with — my husband clearly believed all that fragile goodwill would come crashing to the ground the second I stuck my nose in where it didn't belong.

However, I had no intention of sitting this one out. Josie was one of my best friends, and I knew I'd do whatever it took to make sure she was exonerated and the real killer sent to prison for the rest of his — or her — miserable life.

"Already my plan," I said with a smile, and Brett nodded and slumped against the back of his chair, as though now that he knew I had his aunt's back, he could let himself relax a little.

On my other side, Calvin shook his head slightly, although I could tell he wasn't going to say anything on the subject. Maybe after we got home, he'd try to convince me that locking horns with Henry Lewis once again wasn't the best idea in the world, but it seemed clear he wasn't going to start an argument, not with that deputy sitting at his desk only a few feet away and almost certainly listening to everything we said.

"Did Josie give you any details when she called you?" I asked next. "I mean, did she say what killed Aaron Galloway?"

"No," Brett replied. "She just told me that he died about a half hour after he was brought to the hospital, and that Henry said there was physical evidence connecting her to his death. But she didn't tell me anything more than that."

What kind of physical evidence? Definitely not a smoking gun; Josie didn't even own one, and it seemed pretty obvious that whatever had killed Pastor Galloway, it wasn't a bullet.

He'd complained of stomach pain and then doubled over in agony. Poison, maybe?

I turned toward Calvin. He had a degree in criminology and had taken a class on poisons and other toxic substances that might be used to commit mayhem, and so I knew he had that sort of information stored firmly in his oh-so-capable brain cells. "What kind of poison causes stomach cramps?"

"Lots of them," he said. Something in his posture and his tone seemed almost resigned, as if he'd already known I'd want to pick his brain on the subject...and also knew he couldn't do much about it. "Stomach discomfort is one of the most common reactions to swallowing a toxic substance."

"But something that would kill a person so quickly?" I persisted.

He shrugged. "Hard to say without some pretty in-depth toxicological tests. I'm sure those tests will be part of the post-mortem, so it's mostly a case of waiting to see what the medical examiner has to say."

"That can take weeks, though," I said. Once upon a time, I wouldn't have known quite so much about the timeline for such things—I'd never been one to watch police procedurals or read mysteries—but Danny Ortega's death by accidental poisoning had taught me more than I wanted to know about the procedures that were followed when someone died under mysterious circumstances after ingesting an unknown toxin.

"I'm sure they'll do what they can to expedite things," Calvin said. "But yes, it might take a while."

A time during which Josie would be under a cloud of suspicion. True, anyone who really knew her would also know she couldn't have possibly murdered Aaron Galloway, but at the same time, this whole mess could definitely hurt her real estate business.

And what about her position as mayor?

Would she be able to remain in office, or would she have to step down?

I really didn't want to think about that. She was full of plans to bring some much-needed improvements to the town and do whatever she could to make life better for the people who called it home, and I doubted she'd be able to accomplish much with the specter of such a gruesome crime hanging over her head.

No, the obvious solution was to uncover the real murderer so she'd be able to go on with her life.

Because I'd solved a rough half-dozen murders since coming to Globe, this prospect didn't seem quite as daunting as it once might have. At the same time, though, I knew I'd be facing difficulties when investigating Aaron Galloway's death that I'd never had to deal with before. For one thing, I hadn't even known the victim. Yes, I'd had that brief, uncomfortable encounter with him at Memorial Park, and I'd seen him on those YouTube videos, but that still didn't constitute anything more than the very slightest of acquaintances. For another, he'd been in charge of a large and powerful organization, a group of people I guessed would be all too quick to close ranks if a hedgewitch like me came poking around.

That didn't mean I was entirely without

resources, though. I had my Tarot cards and my pendulum, and the spirit of Grandma Ellen to consult if things got extra dicey. I'd just have to be more cautious than usual.

And at the same time, move as quickly as I could. I had no idea how long Chelsea Haven or the other people from Life Springs Church planned to hang around in Globe, but I had to believe they'd all be gone just as soon as Aaron Galloway's body was released from the coroner's office and on its way back to wherever he'd lived so he could be properly buried.

Something else I needed to find out. There was so much I didn't know about the man.

A rustle just beyond the deputy's front desk made me look up. Henry Lewis was approaching our little group, his brow creased in the sort of furrow that didn't bode well for our future interactions.

Before he could speak, though, I stood up and said, "We're here to post Josie's bail."

"The judge denied bail," Henry replied, his tone curt.

"What?" Brett demanded as he leapt to his feet. "That's ridiculous! My aunt isn't a flight risk."

"Maybe not," Henry returned, looking irritatingly imperturbable. "But the judge ruled that the nature of the crime means she needs to stay in jail until her trial."

Now Calvin also rose from his chair. In contrast to Brett, he looked calm and completely in control, but I could tell from the tightness of his jaw that he wasn't too happy with Henry Lewis—or the unknown judge, whoever he was —right now.

"That doesn't make a lot of sense," Calvin said, tone as measured as his expression. "Josie Woodrow's never had so much as a speeding ticket in her life. And now the judge has denied her bail?"

"She's being held on suspicion of first-degree murder," Henry replied. He also sounded calm, but the narrowing in his cold gray eyes told me he was in no mood to justify his or the judge's actions. "Which is a capital crime, and therefore the judge is within his rights."

"Can we at least talk to her?" I asked desperately. It seemed clear to me Henry wasn't going to budge on this one—not that even he would be able to countermand a judge's orders—but if I couldn't have a few minutes with Josie to see if she had any additional information I could use to help her, then I was sunk before I even got started.

For a long moment, Henry was silent. Since I knew he was no dummy, he'd probably guessed that I wanted to have a convo with Josie so I could start gathering any evidence I could find to prove her evidence.

"She can have one visitor," he said, his gaze moving toward Brett. "One visitor, fifteen minutes."

Oh, boy. I also glanced at Brett, and then waited to hear what he had to say. Yes, it was imperative that I visit Josie and get as many facts from her as I could, but Brett was her family. If he wanted to be the one to go in and talk to her, then I certainly wasn't going to get in the way.

But he seemed to realize that freeing Josie was paramount, because he said, "You go in, Selena. Calvin and I can wait for you out here."

I wasn't about to release a relieved breath, not with Henry standing there and watching me out of those gimlet eyes, but the worried knot in the pit of my stomach seemed to lessen ever so slightly.

"Okay," I said, and faced Henry Lewis. "I'll talk to Josie now, please."

He didn't respond except for a very small tilt of his head. Then he turned and began walking toward the rear of the police station where the jail cells and the facility's single visiting room were located.

As I went, I did my best to keep my head up

high and not make eye contact with anyone. Actually, that was easier today than it might have been under ordinary circumstances, since the station wasn't as heavily staffed on Sundays as it was during the week, and there weren't many deputies around.

Henry led me to the visiting room and told me to take a seat. "I'll have a deputy bring her in. Remember, fifteen minutes."

I nodded.

His gaze moved toward the purse I had slung over one shoulder. "I assume you don't have any nail files in there."

"Nope," I said cheerfully. "Just my phone and my wallet and some lipstick. Oh, and some Tampax."

If possible, his expression grew even more pinched, but he only gave me a brief nod before heading out.

Since I didn't know what else to do, I went ahead and took a seat at the small rectangular table at the center of the space. Since we were just in Globe's tiny jail and not in a real prison, it wasn't like this was a true visiting room with Plexiglas separating the prisoners from their visitors. No, this looked like the kind of place where someone might meet with their lawyer, bare and plain, containing only the single table with its scratched faux woodgrain top and a couple of equally battered chairs flanking it.

A few minutes later, the door opened again. This time, a deputy entered, bringing Josie with him.

I hadn't expected that they'd put her in an orange jumpsuit, but they had. Her short-cropped, fiery hair was only a few shades darker than the jumpsuit itself, and it already seemed as though the makeup she'd been wearing earlier in the day had faded away—or maybe they'd made her take it off. Either way, she looked very pale and tired, and nothing like her usual ebullient self.

Her hands were confined in cuffs, and I sent a sharp look at the deputy. "Are those really necessary?"

"Sorry, ma'am," he said, and he did appear genuinely contrite. I didn't recognize him; he looked very young, maybe no more than twenty-three or twenty-four, and probably hadn't been working for the Globe P.D. for very long. "Standard procedure."

Of course it was. "Well, can she at least sit down?"

"Sure," he replied. "But Chief Lewis told me to remind you that you only have fifteen minutes."

"I haven't forgotten," I said crisply. How

could I, when someone kept reminding me of that cold fact every time I turned around?

The deputy nodded toward Josie, who'd remained uncharacteristically quiet this entire time, and she took the one remaining chair so she could face me across the table. I sent a significant glance at the deputy, and he got the hint right away and hurried from the room.

As soon as he was gone, Josie burst out, "Selena, you have to help me!"

"I will," I said. Seeing her like this had shaken me more than I wanted to admit to myself—Josie had always been such a force of nature that it was hard to see her looking so helpless—but I knew we needed to attend to the task at hand before we ran out of precious time. "First off, do you have a lawyer?"

"No," she replied, looking even more deflated. "That is, I have a lawyer on retainer for my real estate business, but he doesn't handle criminal matters."

"Don't worry," I told her. "I'll have Calvin reach out to the San Ramon tribe's attorney. I'm sure he'll have some recommendations for us. Consider it handled."

"Thank you, Selena," Josie replied. She made a restless movement, and the restraints on her wrists gave an uneasy clink. "I cannot *believe* I am being subjected to this!"

I couldn't either, but the time for righteous indignation would be after we'd discovered Aaron Galloway's real murderer and Josie had been set free. "It stinks, I know," I said. "For now, though, you need to tell me what Henry said at your arraignment. Every little clue might help."

She released a breath. "The preliminary conclusion from the doctors who treated Pastor Galloway is that it was arsenic. They have to do a lot of tests, but I guess his symptoms and the way he died so quickly seemed to point in that direction. They said the arsenic must have been in the coffee he drank just before he died." A pause, and then she said heavily, "The coffee *I* gave him."

Right. I remembered how Josie had told me about going in search of the coffee and then finding it sitting in a carry container backstage at the revival meeting. "You weren't the only person with access to that coffee, though," I replied. "Didn't you say it had been sitting basically abandoned backstage?"

At once, her light blue eyes snapped with indignation, and she looked a little more like the Josie I knew and loved.

"Yes, I did," she exclaimed. "And I told Henry the same thing. I told him plenty of other people could have had access to that coffee and that pretty much anyone could have put the arsenic in it."

"And what did he say?"

Now she seemed to deflate again, and let out a heavy sigh. "He told me that might be true, but none of those other people had a motive like mine."

I lifted an eyebrow. "What motive?" I demanded. "You didn't even know the man."

"No, but his church had just cheated the town out of tens of thousands of dollars."

Oh, that.

Before I could say anything, she went on, "Brand-new mayor...huge scandal...Henry seems to think it was enough to push me over the edge."

"Well, that's just ridiculous," I said indignantly, even as I reflected that Henry Lewis must not be a very good judge of character if he could think a woman he'd known for decades was capable of suddenly snapping like that and killing Aaron Galloway out of anger for the position he'd put her in.

Then again, I supposed one could argue that the jails were full of people who'd "snapped," and that was why the news always seemed to be filled with clips of neighbors and friends shaking their heads and saying that someone had always been quiet and polite, and how they couldn't understand how they were capable of such violence.

Even so, I thought Henry was making a titanic stretch right here.

"I know," Josie said. "I told him I'd already worked it out with Chelsea Haven, and even if I hadn't, I would have simply had the city attorney take Life Springs Church to court to get our money back. Why, I wouldn't know how to get my hands on some arsenic even if I did want to use it on someone." She paused there and lifted an eyebrow at me. "Do *you* know where arsenic comes from?"

"No, I don't," I replied, even as I thought Calvin should be able to tell me. "And this is the sort of thing that'll come out in court...not that I plan to let things get that far."

"I should think not," she returned, again looking more like her old self despite her mussed hair and lack of makeup. "I have faith in you, Selena. I know you'll figure it out in no time."

About all I could do was smile at her as best I could.

Josie Woodrow seemed to have supreme confidence in me.

I just hoped that confidence wasn't misplaced.

7

Arsenic and Old Waste

As soon as I emerged into the police station's waiting room, both Brett and Calvin rose from their chairs.

"How is she?" Brett asked eagerly. "Is she going to be okay?"

"Everything's going to be fine," I said, then sent a sideways glance at the deputy at the front desk. He seemed to be absorbed in something on his computer screen—maybe playing Solitaire, since the station appeared to be dead quiet on that particular Sunday afternoon—but I didn't think having this conversation in front of him was such a good idea. "How about we head outside?"

Brett appeared to take the hint, because he nodded and allowed me to lead him and Calvin out to the parking lot. Once there, I sent a longing glance down the street in the direction of Cloud Coffee, but they were only open until noon on Sundays.

However, Olamendi's was just a block away, and it seemed as good a place for a council of war as anything. "I think we should all go for a drink," I said firmly. "Margaritas?"

Calvin sent me an askance look, and Brett appeared almost startled. After a pause, though, he said, "Okay, sure. We probably need to talk anyway."

Exactly my plan. At three o'clock on a Sunday, the little Mexican restaurant wasn't exactly overflowing with patrons, which was fine by me. Not that we had anything to hide, but I also didn't want to broadcast that I was planning to dive into yet another murder investigation.

Rosa, one of the restaurant's owners, led us to a table in a corner. Maybe she'd picked up on our vibe, or maybe she figured we might as well sit there since it was one of the better spots in the restaurant, about as secluded as you were going to get in a place that was basically one big square room. After we placed our drink orders—margaritas on the rocks for Calvin and me and a mango version for Brett—she headed off to the kitchen to fetch us some chips and salsa and to put in our drink order with her husband, who was the establishment's mixologist.

Since we were alone for the moment, I said, "Josie says it was arsenic."

Brett's eyes widened a bit, but Calvin nodded. "Makes sense, considering the little I've heard about the pastor's symptoms."

I asked the question that had been bothering me ever since I'd heard from Josie how Aaron Galloway had actually died. "How would someone get their hands on enough arsenic to poison someone like that?"

My husband couldn't answer right away, because Rosa and her daughter showed up just then with chips and salsa, glasses of water, and the all-important margaritas. After I assured Rosa that we were only noshing and probably weren't going to order anything else, the two women headed back to the kitchen, leaving the three of us alone again.

As soon as they were gone, Calvin said, "Arsenic used to be used in some fertilizers and paint pigments, but it's been banned for a while. And it's not like cyanide, which you can extract from plant seeds, like apple or grapefruit. About the only thing I can think of is that arsenic is a by-product in some mining processes, so I suppose you could get your hands on it from that source."

Was it a coincidence that Globe had a large copper mine on its western border?

I somehow didn't think so.

While I knew Josie hadn't poisoned Aaron Galloway, I also knew someone else must have done the deed…and it sure sounded as though the culprit had a ready source of the poison he needed right here in our little town.

Calvin must have guessed which direction my thoughts were heading, because he said, "You think they got the arsenic from the Freeport mine."

"Where else?" I asked. "It makes the most sense, doesn't it?"

He picked up his margarita on the rocks and took a sip. "Maybe. I mean, it's not like you can just go into one of their smelters and start scraping the residue off the sides. For one thing, Freeport has some pretty tight security."

I'd never been to the mine, although one of my friends here in Globe, Jennifer Espinoza, was an administrative assistant in Freeport's main office. However, since even I knew people often stole copper by digging up wires and engaging in various other petty crimes, I had to believe the Freeport mine had plenty of security on hand to make sure no one got the idea that they could easily get hold of their much more accessible stores of the precious metal.

"Maybe," I allowed. "But still, it wouldn't be impossible. It could be that the killer bribed one of the mine's employees to get access to the arsenic from the smelter."

Brett reached for a tortilla chip and munched on it moodily. "If that's your theory, though, it's possible Chief Lewis thought the same thing… and that's another reason why he went after my aunt. I mean, she knows tons of people at the mine."

Hmm. I hadn't thought of that angle. It was true that Josie seemed to know just about everyone in Globe, and equally true that, except for her few detractors, pretty much everyone liked and trusted her. There was a reason why she'd run for mayor uncontested; it was pretty much an accepted fact that any opponent facing her in the race would have suffered a crushing defeat, and so no one had bothered. While I still couldn't quite understand how Henry could possibly believe Josie was guilty, he must have reasoned to himself that there were plenty of people who worked at Freeport who'd be willing to give her some smelter scrapings. She could have claimed they were for an art project, or possibly to make custom fertilizer for her garden. After all, Calvin had told me just a minute earlier that arsenic once was used both in paint and fertilizer. It might not have seemed too strange that Josie might request such a thing, since she loved to putter around the house during those rare moments when she wasn't working.

And I had to admit that I was glad my friend Hazel, a local artist of some renown, and her husband Chuck were safely away on their honeymoon in Cozumel, and therefore at least she couldn't be a suspect. I knew she sometimes mixed her own pigments to get a particular effect she couldn't achieve with store-bought paints, and so it didn't seem too unlikely that she might have known how to use arsenic for those sorts of projects. But since she'd been a thousand miles away at the time of the murder, no one would have any reason to believe she might be involved.

"Well, I'm sure Henry is already asking questions," Calvin said as he snagged a tortilla chip of his own. "And will be asking even more tomorrow, when the mine's office staff is back at work. With any luck, no one will know anything, and they'll end up having to dismiss the case due to lack of evidence."

That would definitely be the best possible outcome...for Josie, if not the church...and yet I somehow doubted it would be quite so easy. Henry Lewis was like a bulldog when it came to crimes committed on his watch, and he wouldn't let this go until he had someone permanently behind bars for committing Aaron Galloway's murder. Since this was yet another very public crime with a victim who, if not a household name, was still a celebrity in a lot of circles, there was no way Globe's chief of police was going to let the world think you could get away with murder in his town.

And while I knew Henry was good at his job and not the kind of man who would necessarily take the path of least resistance, I also knew he wasn't the sort to start exploring strange leads when he already had a perfectly plausible subject locked up in jail and awaiting trial.

Which meant the ball was firmly in my court.

"And I've got a lot of questions of my own," I said, then paused so I could take a much-delayed sip of my margarita. "When we get home after this, I'm going to give Jennifer Espinoza a call. She's usually home on Sundays because that's when she does most of her housework."

At least Jennifer's weekends weren't all cleaning toilets and doing laundry these days. Late in September, she'd started dating a man who lived in Gilbert, someone she'd met online. While I didn't know whether I would've had the intestinal fortitude to go looking for love on a dating site, it seemed she'd lucked out. The only real downside was that if things got serious, I had no doubt she'd leave Globe to move in with her boyfriend. There wasn't much to attract a person to Globe unless they had money of their own or wanted to work for the mine, and since it sounded as though her current squeeze had a good-paying job as an HVAC repairman, he probably would want to stay put. After all, there were thousands and thousands of air conditioners in the greater Phoenix area that needed regular tending.

"Do you really think Jennifer would know that much?" Calvin asked. He'd made serious inroads on the basket of tortilla chips and now looked a little worried that Rosa might not come back to give us a refill before we'd all finished our drinks and it was time to go. "I thought she worked in the main office at Freeport and didn't have much to do with what actually goes on in the mine."

"She does," I said. "But she's been there for almost seven years. I don't think it matters that she spends most of her time handling paperwork and making phone calls. She's still been around the mine and the people who run it for a long time, and she's a smart woman. I'll bet she's picked up all kinds of useful information."

Brett had been listening to Calvin's and my

back-and-forth, and gave a sage nod. "I think you're right, Selena," he said. "I'm sure she'll have some good input."

"Well, I'll drink to that," Calvin said, and we all solemnly clinked our margarita glasses.

Since it appeared we'd settled on my next course of action, there didn't seem to be much to do except finish our margaritas and the basket of tortilla chips, and then head for home. Brett appeared worried, of course, but also glad I was on the case. Clearly, he put a lot more faith in my sleuthing skills than he did in Henry Lewis's ability to bring the real killer to justice.

And I couldn't really blame him. When it came to tracking down murderers, so far I had a lot more notches on my belt than Chief Lewis.

Sadie was rapturously glad to see Calvin and me, even though we'd only been gone for a few hours. She was just fine being on her own for parts of the day, since he'd installed an automatic dog door for her in the laundry room, one that opened onto an enclosed dog run we'd put together on the side of the house. It had grass and a small doghouse in case she wanted to sit outside for a while and listen to all the various sounds and smell all the scents carried on the wind.

But even though she'd been granted such luxury, it didn't compare to having her people around. Calvin scooped her up and ruffled her ears while she did her best to lick his chin. Despite my worry for Josie, I couldn't help smiling a little.

"The dog must think you taste good," I commented, and Calvin shot me a grin.

"I probably do," he replied. "I'm sure I got some salt on there while I was eating tortilla chips."

"True," I said with a grin. "You were macking down on those pretty hard. I'm surprised you left any for Brett and me."

Being Calvin, my husband didn't respond to the lighthearted barb, but only lifted one eyebrow a fraction of an inch. "I'll watch some TV while you call Jennifer," he said. "You were going to call her, right?"

"That's the plan," I responded. Although the afternoon felt as though it had lasted for roughly a hundred years, it was just a little past five, which meant we had plenty of time before our dinner reservations at seven o'clock. I couldn't recall a time when I'd felt less like heading over to the Gold Dust casino's restaurant for a steak dinner, but I hoped I'd be more in the mood after I talked to Jennifer. "I'll go in my office to make the call so I won't disturb you."

He nodded, and I headed down the hall to the room I'd taken over as my own. For just a second, Sadie looked as though she wanted to follow me, but then she appeared to decide against it...probably because Calvin was known to graze as he sat in front of the TV, while I never brought food into my office. Since my altar was in there, it felt somehow disrespectful to be munching away on a snack in a place that was supposed to be sacred.

I slipped my purse off my shoulder and slung it on the back of the old-fashioned wooden rolling chair I kept at my desk, then reached into the bag and pulled out my phone. No missed calls, which meant Josie hadn't been given a miraculous reprieve while Calvin and Brett and I discussed strategy and drank margaritas.

Probably, such an outcome was way too much to ask for, but a girl could hope.

I found Jennifer Espinoza's number in my contacts list and then touched the screen to connect the call. As I sat there and listened to her phone ring, I worried that maybe she really was busy, that she'd headed out to Walmart to get in some last-minute shopping before her week started, or she'd decided to head over to Gilbert to go to the movies with her boyfriend. However, just before the call was about to roll over to voicemail, she picked up, sounding breathless.

"Hi, Selena," she said. "You caught me in the middle of unloading some laundry. What's up?"

Well, at least I didn't have to worry about interrupting her in the middle of a date or something. "Have you heard about Josie?" I asked.

I couldn't see Jennifer's expression, but something told me it sobered abruptly. "I did," she said. "Terry called me about an hour ago. It's awful!"

The two women had been classmates at Globe High and had maintained their friendship over the intervening fifteen years, so it didn't seem too strange to me that Brett's wife would have called Jennifer to let her know what was going on. And if Terry hadn't called, I had no doubt someone else would have. The grapevine in my adopted hometown seemed better most days than any CIA spy network.

"It is," I agreed. "And I'm trying to help her out. Do you mind if I ask you a few questions?"

"Not at all," Jennifer replied. "Anything to clear Josie's name. What do you need to know?"

"How hard would it be to get arsenic from the residue left inside one of your company's smelters?"

A pause. Then Jennifer said, "Is that what killed Pastor Galloway? Arsenic?"

"Early signs say so," I told her. "I mean, it's

way too soon for a real toxicological test to have come back, but judging by his symptoms and how quickly he died, Calvin says it makes sense."

She didn't ask how Calvin could have known such a thing. He might not have been Globe's police chief, but everyone in town at least knew something about him in passing, including that he'd gone to Arizona State in Tempe to get his criminology degree.

Another of those hesitations, and then Jennifer said, "I honestly don't know how easy it would be to get arsenic out of any of the tailings or smelter residue at our mine. There are tons of regulations in place to make sure we scrub as much of it as possible, so it's not as if we've got a bunch of arsenic-heavy tailings— the residue left over after we've extracted the ore—just sitting out there waiting for someone to pick them up and extract the heavy metals they contain."

I supposed I should have thought of that. What I knew about the mining industry could probably fit on the head of a pin, but I'd never heard of the Freeport mine getting fined for any kind of environmental safety violations. If they were as squeaky-clean as Jennifer made them sound, then they couldn't have been the source of the arsenic the killer had used to ensure Aaron Galloway moved on to his just rewards.

And if that was the case, then I'd just gotten sent right back to square one.

"Still," I persisted, not quite ready to give up this particular theory, "is there any chance at all that someone might have access to those tailings before they get cleaned up?"

"Maybe," Jennifer said slowly, her dubious tone telling me she thought this line of questioning was a dead end. "I mean, we have people on staff who inspect all the mitigation equipment, so I suppose it's just slightly possible that one of them would be able to get in there and collect some of the contaminated rocks and other residue."

That seemed the most likely explanation. Of course, having access didn't mean any of those people had an axe to grind with Pastor Galloway. Then again, in their case, this probably hadn't been about revenge, but just getting some money slipped under the table to them for something the higher-ups at the mine would never miss.

"Do you know their names?" I asked. Maybe this was all one horribly long shot, but I had to start somewhere.

"Um…Mark Lemmon," Jennifer replied. "He's the chief inspector for all the environmental stuff at the mine. And he has two guys working for him—Ross Davison and Brian Vaughn."

"Do they all live here in Globe?"

"Mark does," Jennifer said. "I think Ross and Brian live over in Miami."

That improbably named little town was just the other side of the hill from the mine, and had a cost of living even lower than Globe, which was probably why the two technicians lived there. But Miami was close enough that heading over there and asking a few leading questions wouldn't take too much of my time.

The much harder part would be getting either Ross or Brian to talk to me in the first place. There wasn't much reason why the owner of a New Age store would need to discuss something with them...unless, of course, one of them was an accessory to the crime and would guess right away the motive behind such a conversation.

"Do you know their schedules?" I inquired next. It might take me a little while to come up with a plausible excuse for reaching out to any of the three men, but it couldn't hurt to know when I might be able to pin them down, just in case.

"Um, Mark does a standard eight-to-five, Monday through Friday," she said. "I think Ross works weekends, so he'd have Monday-Tuesday off. I can't remember Brian's schedule off-hand —I'll have to look it up when I go in to the office tomorrow morning."

That would have to do. Since Mark would be at work most of the week, he might be a little harder to pin down, but if Ross was fancy-free both tomorrow and Tuesday, it shouldn't be too difficult to slip off and have a little convo with him.

Well, except for one thing....

"I don't suppose you know Ross's address," I said.

"Not off the top of my head," Jennifer said. "I'd just try Googling him—he's not the sort of person who would do much to hide his personal information. It's in the database at work, but I could get fired if anyone found out I'd passed that info along to you."

The last thing I wanted was to get Jennifer in trouble. She'd already been enormously helpful, and so I knew I needed to take the information she'd given me and see what I could do with it on my own.

"No worries," I said hastily. "I'll figure it out. Like you said, this whole angle might be a real long shot, but I need to start somewhere."

"I wish I could do more," Jennifer replied. "This thing with Josie is just awful. I still can't believe Henry Lewis would think she had anything to do with it."

The phrase "convenient scapegoat" floated through my head, but I didn't want to be quite that uncharitable. Henry could only work with the data he had, and for the moment, that data was pointing at Josie.

"We'll fix it," I said. "Don't worry."

"I sure hope so. You have a good evening, Selena."

I wished the same to Jennifer, and we hung up. As I returned my phone to my purse, however, I had a feeling this was going to be anything but easy.

8

Dirty Work

WELL, JENNIFER HAD BEEN RIGHT ABOUT ONE thing. As far as I could tell, Ross Davison hadn't done a darn thing to obfuscate his online identity. He owned a small house not too far off Highway 60, had worked for the Freeport mine for the past five years, and, at almost exactly thirty, was a year and a half younger than I was.

That morning at the store, I filled Archie in about what had happened the day before. Because the residents of Globe still viewed him as something of a newcomer, he wasn't as connected to the town's grapevine as a lot of people, and so he'd missed out on all the drama.

Or maybe his cluelessness had more to do with Victoria being here all weekend, leaving Archie blissfully unaware of pretty much everything around him except her presence.

Luckily, he was still sporting the afterglow from her visit, and so he expressed his disbelief over Josie's arrest, made a few pointed comments about Henry Lewis's thick head, and didn't give me too much grief about leaving him in charge of the shop while I drove over to Miami to talk to Ross Davison.

Of course, being Archie, he still couldn't quite resist throwing a few caveats my way.

"What if he's not home?" he asked. Since it was a Monday morning, we weren't exactly what one could call busy, and so he had a rag in one hand and had been keeping himself occupied with wiping away whatever minuscule amounts of dust might have collected on the crystals and books and other odds and ends during the weekend.

"Then I'll come back to work and try again tomorrow," I said imperturbably. "Jennifer told me Ross has today and tomorrow off, so this isn't my only chance."

Archie gave a very slight nod in response to my reply, and ran the rag over a line of paperbacks on one of the bookshelves. "And you really think he'll have anything of note to tell you?"

"Maybe he will, maybe he won't," I responded. "Right now, though, this is my only lead, and so I'd be stupid not to follow it. The sooner I get to the bottom of this, the sooner Josie will be out of jail."

"I suppose that's true," he said. He stopped there, dark gold eyebrows drawing together slightly. "She must be furious with Henry."

"Oh, definitely," I agreed. And, while I was certainly not an advocate for giving in to your anger, I had to admit that in this case, Josie's fury was a good thing. Being angry might help to keep her from being worried and scared.

I just had to hope her anger would be enough to sustain her until I could get this mess figured out.

"Anyway," I went on, "I shouldn't be gone for more than an hour or an hour and a half at the most. Just hold down the fort until I get back."

Archie sent a sardonic glance around the empty shop. Even with Christmas looming a month away, we weren't exactly being overrun with shoppers. "I'll do my best."

I sent him a grateful smile and headed out back so I could get in my Jeep. A moment of fiddling with the nav so I could get Ross Davison's address entered into it, and then I was on my way. By that point it was around ten-thirty, far past Globe's modest morning rush hour, so I made good time. As I drove, I did my best to rehearse what I might say to Mr. Davison that would convince him I wasn't a complete madwoman.

Presenting myself as a good friend of Josie Woodrow's seemed to be the best course of action. After all, I was following up a lead I'd gotten in the most normal way possible—from talking with a friend—and so it wasn't as though I'd have to try explaining away any clues I might have found thanks to my Tarot cards or a propitious swing of my favorite fluorite pendulum.

Although Miami was pretty much right next door to Globe in the grand scheme of things, I'd never spent much time there, had only viewed it as a place to pass through on my way to Gilbert or Mesa or whatever suburb of Phoenix I might be headed to in order to do some shopping or run other errands. I was actually surprised to see that Miami's downtown was almost as cute as Globe's, although it wasn't in quite as good repair and appeared to be in the middle of some fairly extensive restoration to some of its buildings, judging by all the scaffolding I saw.

Ross Davison's house was located toward the north end of town, on a quiet street of homes that looked as though they'd probably been built in the same late 1940s/early 1950s postwar boom that had seen the creation of hundreds of similar houses in Globe. His was a small Spanish-style home with a front yard of cactus and gravel and not much else, and the utter lack of flowerpots or any other kind of personal touch told me he probably lived here alone.

The house had a carport, not a garage. A dusty dark blue Chevy Silverado pickup was parked there, telling me Ross probably was home. There really wasn't much of interest within walking distance—as far as I was able to tell, anyway—and so I sort of doubted the truck would be here if he wasn't.

I drove a little ways down the street, and then turned around and parked in front of his neighbor two doors down. Maybe I was being overly cautious, but it just seemed a good idea not to stop right in front of Ross Davison's house. This way, even if he'd been looking out the window for some reason, my arrival shouldn't arouse too much suspicion.

The day was cool but bright, just like so many other November days in our part of the world. Anticipating this meeting, I'd dressed a little more casually than I otherwise might have, in jeans and low-heeled boots and a burgundy sweater. Nothing about my appearance screamed out that I was the owner of a New Age store, and that was exactly how I wanted it. Yes, Ross might know who I was by name, but I had a feeling he wouldn't recognize me by sight, giving me a slight advantage here.

I mounted the two steps to the modest front porch. No doorbell in sight, and so I lifted my hand and knocked.

No answer. I glanced around, but the neighborhood was quiet, with most of its residents probably off at work or at school. What if I'd come too early? Yes, it was eleven o'clock in the morning, but maybe Mr. Davison slept in on his days off, or maybe he was awake but in the shower. Or —

The door opened, and Ross Davison blinked down at me, clearly startled. He was tall and gangly, with messy dark brown hair and muddy hazel eyes. A bemused rub of his hand against the bristles on his chin, and then he said, "Can I help you?"

"Hi," I replied, doing my best to sound pleasant and cheery…but not *too* cheery. It was a Monday morning, after all, and I wasn't here selling Avon. "I'm Selena Marx. Could I talk to you for a minute or two?"

Instead of looking even more confused, the way I'd expected, Ross Davison said, "Oh…

you're the woman who solves all those murders, right?"

Should I be flattered that I was known for something more than selling crystals and books and doing the occasional Tarot reading?

"Yep, that's me," I said brightly. "Do you have time for a quick chat?"

"Sure," he said, and then backed out of the way so I could come inside.

As I entered the small living room, whose main decorative feature appeared to be the shoes on the floor and the empty pizza box on the coffee table, a small flicker of fear trickled its way down my spine. Was it really smart for me to have come by myself to a strange man's house? Maybe I should've closed down the shop altogether and brought Archie along as backup.

But then Ross apologized for the mess and invited me to sit down, even as he gathered up the pizza box and kicked a pair of work boots under the couch. Then he asked if I wanted a glass of water or something.

"No, I'm fine," I said, then sat down in the spot he'd indicated. The sofa had definitely seen better days, but at least there weren't any obvious food stains on the cushion where I'd settled myself.

"Are you here about a murder?" Ross asked, his tone almost eager.

"Actually, yes," I responded. "Did you hear about what happened to Aaron Galloway?"

"That preacher guy who was coming to speak in Globe?"

I nodded.

"Nope," Ross said, still looking way too cheerful, considering the reason for my visit. "I went pretty much straight to bed after I got off shift last night, and I don't listen to the news."

Which had already picked up the story. At least, the Phoenix outlets had. They reported it as developing news and promised more details on the afternoon broadcast, a promise they obviously intended to keep, since I'd passed several news vans as I was heading out of town this morning.

Well, this time I probably wouldn't have to worry about dodging reporters, since I was only tangentially connected to Aaron Galloway's murder, and therefore they had no reason to talk to me.

"He died yesterday," I said. "The doctors are guessing it was arsenic."

For all his sloppy appearance, it seemed Ross Davison was no dummy. His expression grew somehow still, and he said, "And you think someone got it from the mine."

It was a statement, not a question, but I

answered anyway. "That's my theory," I replied. "I mean, Freeport's the most obvious place to get arsenic around here, isn't it?"

"I suppose so," Ross said. He stopped there to ruffle the over-long hair at the back of his head as a frown pulled at his heavy brows. At least, I assumed he was frowning; anyone with eyebrows and a nose like that always looked at least a little concerned. "It wouldn't be easy, though. I mean, we've got video surveillance everywhere, and those parts of the mines need a key card for access."

The place sounded like a regular Fort Knox. But then, I supposed I shouldn't be too surprised by all the security measures in place at the Freeport facility, since they weren't exactly mining Play-Doh over there.

"But if they had someone at the mine helping them?" I asked.

"Maybe," Ross said. His thin lips quirked a little, and he added, "If you're trying to exonerate your friend, that's probably not the angle you want to take, though. I mean, I don't know her personally, but Josie Woodrow has lots of contacts at Freeport. She would be a more likely suspect than a lot of people around here."

Well, he had me there. Except....

"Can you think of anyone you work with

who would've had a grudge against Aaron Galloway?" I inquired next. Maybe it was a long shot, but I needed to do whatever I could to direct the investigation toward someone other than my friend.

Ross's thin shoulders lifted. He was wearing a ratty-looking Arizona Cardinals T-shirt and cargo shorts, and clearly hadn't planned to go anywhere special on his day off. "Not really," he said. "But it's not like we talk about religion at work. We mostly talk sports or about work-related stuff."

That didn't surprise me too much. In any environment where people needed to get along with each other on a daily basis, politics and religion were the two subjects everyone tended to avoid.

Still, I wasn't about to give up my theory quite so easily. "No one at all?"

He paused for a moment, then shrugged again. "One of the guys made a crack about his wife sending too much money to one of those TV preachers, but I don't know who he was talking about. Anyway, he sounded more amused than anything, like a guy complaining about how much his wife spends on shoes."

It wasn't a lot to go on, but since I was grasping at straws here....

"Who was it?" I asked, and Ross tilted his head slightly, as if trying to recall the incident.

"Can't remember," he replied. "It was just something they said in passing. It definitely didn't seem like a big deal to me."

Maybe it was, maybe it wasn't. Since he couldn't seem to remember who'd made the remark in the first place, pressing the issue would only be a waste of time.

Figuring I might as well move on, I said, "But if someone who worked there did hold a grudge against Pastor Galloway, could they have gotten their hands on enough arsenic to poison someone?"

Ross looked down at his jeans and rubbed a hand across one worn knee, a gesture I assumed meant he thought it was possible but didn't necessarily want to go on record saying so.

"I don't know about 'probable,'" he said. "But I guess anything's possible." He paused, his hazel eyes now interested, sharp. "How much arsenic do you need to poison somebody, anyway?"

Good question. That was something I'd need to ask Calvin, except I had to believe it couldn't be very much, or Aaron Galloway might have noticed something was off about his coffee. "I have no idea," I said frankly. "But I doubt it takes a lot. So that means if whoever killed the pastor actually did get their arsenic from the mine, then they wouldn't have had to steal very much. They probably could have slipped it into a little baggie and called it a day."

"Then it could've been anyone," Ross replied. "Or at least, anyone who has access to the tailings. There's also a smelter here in Miami, and that would be another place someone could have gotten some scrapings. I know there are a bunch of ways to extract arsenic from that kind of stuff, but it involves the kind of equipment that a regular person wouldn't have."

"But you have that equipment at the mine, don't you?" I asked.

"Yeah," he said, now looking dubious again. "But only a few people know how to operate it. Honestly, it would be a lot of work when all you'd really need to do is go scoop up the arsenic from a landfill."

For a moment, I just stared at him. Such a deadly poison couldn't really be that easy to get...could it?

"You dump toxic substances like that in a landfill?" I demanded.

"We're not doing anything wrong," Ross said, his tone just a touch defensive. "Other companies do the same thing all over America. But yeah, all the arsenic-contaminated tailings go to the Gila County landfill south of Globe."

Right back in my own stomping grounds. I'd never been to the landfill because I'd never had anything to get rid of that would have necessitated such a trip, but I knew the place was only a few miles from downtown Globe.

"Is there a designated area where you dump the mine's toxic waste, or does it just go wherever?" I asked.

Now he shrugged. "I dunno. I'm not in charge of that part of the operation."

"Do you know who is?"

Ross shook his head. "Nope. I could try to find out, though."

I didn't see any reason to have him go to that trouble, not when Jennifer could probably provide me with the same information. Right now, since I had absolutely no idea who the murderer was, I thought it was better to be as discreet as possible. Ross had provided me with some valuable information, especially the part about the arsenic-laden tailings being dumped at the local landfill, but if he started poking around at the mine, he might attract precisely the wrong sort of attention.

"That's fine," I said quickly. "I'll figure it out. You've given me a lot to go on, though. I really appreciate all the help."

I stood up, and he also rose from the threadbare armchair where he'd been sitting. "You're sure you don't need any more help?"

Once again, he wore that almost eager look on his face. I got the impression he didn't have much going on in his life, and helping me play amateur sleuth was just the diversion he'd been looking for.

Problem was, I didn't want to drag anyone else into this. I might have been taking a big enough risk on my own, but that was my decision to make. Besides, I'd survived quite a few of these investigations already and had no reason to believe I wouldn't survive this one, too.

Even if a few of those previous inquiries had led to some *extremely* close calls.

"Thanks so much, Ross," I said. "But I don't want you to attract any negative attention that might get you in trouble at work. It's probably better if I do this on my own."

Disappointment flitted across his sharp, bony features, but to my relief, he didn't try to press the issue. "I get it," he responded. "But if you need anything else, you know where to find me."

I thanked him again and headed out. As I walked down the front path to the spot where my Renegade waited at the curb, I took a quick glance down at myself. I was dressed pretty casually, but I knew my footwear would never hold up to the next stage of my investigation.

No, I needed to head home and change so I'd be ready for some dump-diving.

———

Archie didn't seem too thrilled that I intended to extend my morning's sleuthing activities, but at least he didn't try to outright forbid me to go to the landfill. Actually, he seemed more worried than anything else.

"You're sure that's the sort of place you should be roaming around by yourself?" he asked.

I had the phone call patched through the Jeep's audio system so I wouldn't be too distracted while driving. Eyes still fixed on the bumpy country road ahead of me—I was almost home by now—I replied, "I'll be careful. I'm planning to grab some rubber gloves and one of the respirators Calvin uses when he's painting. That should keep the worst of it off me."

Or so I hoped. I honestly had no idea what people wore when working with arsenic, but I had to hope that covering my hands and my eyes and nose and mouth would be enough to keep me safe. Besides, it wasn't as though I planned to go rolling in the stuff. I just wanted to see if the part of the landfill where they dumped the really toxic waste was something that could be easily accessed, or whether it was hidden behind barbed wire and gates with squads of mean-looking security guards.

Okay, probably not a whole bunch of security guards. I couldn't really see our cash-strapped county springing for that kind of expense.

I pulled up to the front of the house and got out of the car. As soon as I came through the door, Sadie was there, tail wagging while she got on her hind legs and pawed at my jeans.

"Hey, sweetie," I said, bending down so I could scratch her behind her oversized ears. "I'm just popping in to change. You'll need to keep holding down the fort for a bit longer."

She shook and then let out one of her meeping little whines, the kind she generally employed when she was trying to get something out of me or Calvin. It was actually cool enough outside now that I could have left her safely in the Jeep while I roamed around the landfill, and yet I didn't think that was such a great idea. If anything happened to me, then the poor dog would be stuck in the vehicle until someone noticed she was trapped inside.

"No, it's not safe where I'm going," I told her, and patted her on the head. We always spoke to Sadie like she was a regular person, and she really did seem to understand a lot of what we were saying. At any rate, while she looked dejected, she stopped pawing at my leg and instead followed me into the bedroom.

Off went my flats and on went the hiking boots I'd bought not long after moving to Globe, and then I changed out my sweater for a grubby old sweatshirt that Calvin had been about to give away to Goodwill but which I'd snagged out of the donation bag, figuring it would be good to keep on hand for any really dirty chores. The thing reached almost to my knees, but I wasn't worried about winning any beauty contests.

No, I just didn't want to inadvertently give myself arsenic poisoning.

Once arrayed in my dump-diving attire, I headed to the garage to scrounge the gloves and respirator Calvin kept on his workbench. At least that part of the garage was in fairly good order, so they weren't too hard to find. However, I purposely made myself not look at the clutter that filled the rest of the space, since doing so would only make me cranky. There was probably enough stuff in there to fill at least two good-sized storage units, if not more.

Choose your battles, I reminded myself, and went back into the house. Sadie shot me an expectant look, so I got a treat out of the pantry and handed it to her.

"Here you go, sweetie," I said. "Don't let it ruin your lunch."

Her tail wagged, but I could tell from the way one ear drooped that she wasn't thrilled by the bribe. She was great at regulating her food intake, so I always filled her bowl before I left for work, knowing she wouldn't head over to eat her midday meal until noon rolled around. Whoever had trained her before she came into Calvin's and my lives, they'd done a pretty awesome job.

I locked up the house and got back in the Jeep, then looked up the landfill on my nav and let it send me in the direction I needed to go. As I'd vaguely recalled from seeing signs pointing toward the facility, it was almost due south of Globe, although the only way in took me to nearly the western edge of town, where Highway 188 came in from the north.

As I went, I found myself thanking the Goddess for navigation systems. The road in to the landfill —improbably named Hope Lane— twisted and turned, heading up into the hills, and I doubted I would've been able to find it on my own even with a map. However, I knew I was on the right track, because I passed several garbage trucks winding their way back down the hill, as well as a couple of people hauling trailers behind their trucks, people who'd probably gone up to the dump to get rid of yard refuse or oversized items that the regular waste collection people wouldn't have picked up.

A small guard shack sat in the middle of the road where it approached the dump. I slowed my Jeep and came to a stop, then rolled down my window as a man came out of the shack and squinted through the bright sunlight at me. He looked as though he was probably in his late fifties, and wore a dark blue shirt with the Gila County logo printed above the pocket on his left breast.

"Whatcha dumping?" he inquired.

Luckily, I'd already manufactured a lie for just this occasion. "Nothing," I said, doing my best to look worried but utterly innocuous. "I lost my wedding ring, and I realized it must have been in the trash that was picked up this morning. Do you know where it would've been dropped off?"

The man scratched the back of his head. "From this morning? Over on the east side, toward the back." He sent me a pitying look. "That's a lot of garbage to go through."

No kidding. Good thing I had no intention of actually scrabbling through the trash—I just needed a good excuse for why I'd be wandering around here at all.

"I know," I said. "But I've got to look for it. My husband will kill me if he finds out I lost the ring. It cost him two months' salary."

This seemed to be exactly the right tack to take, because the man didn't ask any other questions, only gave me another of those sympathetic glances and pointed in the direction he'd indicated a minute earlier.

"Stay on the roads," he said. "You've got four-wheel drive there, but you'd still be in trouble if you went off course."

"I'll be careful," I promised him.

That definitely wasn't a lie. The Goddess only knew what kind of a reaction I'd get from Calvin if I called him to tow me out of a trash heap.

I went through the gates and followed the road—really, just a dirt lane that ran through the landfill—in the direction the guard had indicated. However, my destination wasn't the spot where that morning's garbage had been dropped off, but whichever area turned out to be the place where the Freeport mine had been dumping its tailings and other assorted toxic waste.

Luckily, the landfill's various zones were fairly

well-marked. As the guard had said, it looked as though everything brought in by the area's trash trucks was dumped off to the east, while yard and other green waste had a section not too far from the entrance. I trundled my Renegade along at a modest five miles an hour, looking from side to side, and then I saw the sign I'd been seeking.

Hazardous Waste.

The arrow pointed toward what the compass of my Jeep said was due south, which made sense. They'd want to dump the really bad stuff as far away from town as possible.

This part of the landfill looked like the terrain of some impossibly hostile planet, with piles of earth in colors that nature had definitely never intended—rusty orange and bile yellow and a particularly nasty acid green—and mounds of dark rocks and gravel that I guessed were the tailings from the mine. At the far end were a bunch of metal barrels with a skull and crossbones sticker on each one and the handy legend "Danger/Peligro" written below it, just in case the death's head logo wasn't indication enough of their contents.

I came to a stop and surveyed the area. It was immediately obvious to me that basically anyone could come in here and scoop up as much of the contaminated soil as they needed, then extract whatever nasties they wanted from it.

Only…Ross had made it sound as though there were some intricate processes involved in actually pulling pure arsenic from mine tailings. Maybe there were, or maybe it was the sort of thing a person could do while using a basic chemistry lab. None of this was my forté, so I had absolutely no idea what might actually be involved in the procedure.

All I knew was that if someone needed to get their hands on a bunch of arsenic-contaminated waste, they'd only have to drive out here, pick up what they needed, and head for home.

Which meant the killer could have been pretty much anyone who knew about the landfill, or who'd done their research.

I let out a sigh.

"Back to square one," I muttered.

Still, I wasn't going to go home completely empty-handed. While I was still at the shop, I'd shoved a couple of small plastic bags—the sort of thing I used to ship jewelry or smaller crystals—into one of the inner pockets of my purse. Now I pulled on the gloves I'd brought along and awkwardly fished them out, figuring I'd bring home a few samples so I could have them tested at a lab to see exactly how much arsenic they contained. If nothing else, I hoped to discover whether or not the tailings here really had high enough levels of the toxin to be viable.

Some of the stink from the landfill made it past the respirator I'd just donned, but not very much. Gingerly, I made my way across the rocky landscape to one of the mounds of tailings and picked up a few rocks and chunks of gravel, and stuck them in a plastic bag. I also collected some of the weird-colored earth below my feet, just because I figured it couldn't hurt to test as many samples as possible to see exactly what we were dealing with out here.

That task done, I headed back to the Jeep and did my best to kick my hiking boots against one of the tires in an attempt to get rid of the toxic dirt that was clinging to them. I definitely didn't want to track any more of that junk into the vehicle than I had to, although I thought I'd better clean out the interior of the car with Calvin's shop vac when I got home, just to be safe.

As I climbed inside, I sent a wary glance around my immediate surroundings, but this part of the landfill was completely deserted. From somewhere off in the distance came the insistent *beep beep beep* of a garbage truck backing up, but they were nowhere near the spot where I'd parked.

Good. I wanted as few witnesses to my expedition out here as possible.

Poisonous earth stowed in my purse, I headed back to town. I still didn't know for sure what I was going to do with it, but I couldn't help hoping I carried with me the key to Josie's freedom.

Because if this all turned out to be a dead end, I wasn't sure what I'd do next.

9

Cold Shoulder

"YOU WENT OUT TO THE LANDFILL?" CALVIN asked, looking incredulous.

We sat at the dining room table, sharing the chili I'd started in the crockpot before I left for work that morning. After I finished my little expedition to the dump, I'd come home, vacuumed out the Jeep, and then immediately stripped down and threw all my clothes—well, except my hiking boots, obviously—into the washing machine. I'd then showered and put on a clean outfit before heading back to the shop. By that point, it was almost one o'clock and Archie was none too thrilled with me for being away almost half the day, but at least I felt as if I'd accomplished something.

Exactly what, however, I wasn't sure.

"I had to," I said simply. "I needed to see

whether the stuff Freeport is dumping out there could have been used to poison Aaron Galloway." I paused and set down my spoon, causing Sadie, who was loitering down near my feet, to slump dejectedly. She loved chili and had obviously been hoping I'd feed her a morsel or two of ground beef. "Is there a way to tell if arsenic has come from a particular source?"

Calvin considered my question for a moment, then shook his head. "I don't think so. Arsenic's a metallic element, so that means it's pure. It would be like trying to figure out where an oxygen molecule came from."

"Oh," I said, my tone flat. It hadn't occurred to me that arsenic was a metal...or an element... but then, I wasn't a chemist.

Or a geologist, even though I sold a lot of crystals in my shop and knew a good bit about their properties and their places of origin. But while it wasn't too difficult to determine where a crystal had come from because of the various elements that gave the stone its particular character, you couldn't say the same thing about a hunk of gold. It was just...gold.

Which meant connecting the arsenic that had been used to kill Aaron Galloway to any particular location would be well-nigh impossible.

My husband seemed to take pity on me, because he said, "But it's possible the arsenic the murderer used wasn't pure. It just had to be concentrated enough to kill him quickly."

"If it wasn't pure, though, shouldn't he have tasted something funky in his coffee?" I asked.

"Maybe, maybe not. It depends on how much other stuff was mixed in. You don't need a lot of arsenic to kill a person."

That particular point was something Calvin had clarified for me while I was putting the finishing touches on dinner and we were hanging out in the kitchen, sharing a pre-meal glass of wine. According to him, the amount of arsenic that constituted a killing dose was very small, only a tiny fraction of an ounce. Even if the killer hadn't been able to extract the pure element to create his poison, the amount of arsenic-laced rock dust needed to ensure Aaron Galloway left this mortal coil post haste was still fairly negligible.

Because I must have looked pretty dejected right then, Calvin added quickly, "But if the arsenic wasn't pure, then those soil traces should show up in the tox tests. At least that would pinpoint where it had come from."

"And point straight back to Josie," I said, feeling even more deflated.

"Not necessarily," my husband replied. "It's not like that section of the landfill is watched too closely—as you just found out. Pretty much anyone could go in there and get what they wanted."

Well, that was true. The mental image of Josie rolling up to the Gila County landfill in her red Cadillac made me smile a little. Even the bored-looking guard at the dump would have taken notice of the new mayor's arrival, which wouldn't exactly be optimal for someone who was trying to work in stealth.

Honestly, Josie Woodrow was the least stealthy person I knew.

"So I should be focusing on motive instead of where the arsenic came from?" I asked, wondering if I'd wasted all that time chasing around today.

"Maybe," Calvin said. "Or at least, I think this is a case where the 'why' might lead you to a quicker solution than trying to figure out the 'how.'"

Probably good advice, but at the moment, I had no idea who would have wanted Aaron Galloway dead, and no real notion of where to start that particular line of questioning.

Except....

"Do you know how long it will take before the medical examiner releases Aaron Galloway's body?" I asked, thinking furiously. Not that I could even pretend to know the woman, but I had to believe Chelsea Haven wouldn't leave Globe until it was time to accompany her boss's remains to their final resting place.

Calvin picked up the ladle and dished some more chili into his bowl. "He died under suspicious circumstances, so it'll definitely take longer than usual…at least three or four days, maybe more. They won't hold him until the toxicology report comes back, because that can take months, but I know the M.E. will still take longer with the autopsy than he would with someone whose death wasn't obviously foul play—like Brant Thoreau."

I did my best not to wince at that casual reference. Brant had died while investigating a possible demon infestation at the Bigelow mansion, the big Victorian house my parents had bought in Globe almost a year and a half ago. It turned out the demons were utterly fake…and that he'd been pushed down the stairs by Al Loomis, the man who'd done the home inspection on the place and who'd been in cahoots with the former head of Globe's chamber of commerce to drive my parents out of the house so the property could be sold to a big development company. At the time, however, Brant's death hadn't appeared to be anything more than a tragic accident.

At any rate, the medical examiner had

released Brant's body fairly quickly after foul play had been ruled out, but in Aaron Galloway's case, it was pretty obvious he'd been poisoned, even if it was going to take a while to figure out exactly how.

Which all worked in my favor. The longer Chelsea Haven stuck around in Globe, the more chance I'd have to talk to her and see if she might be able to provide any tidbits that could lead me to the real killer.

First, though, I'd need to track her down.

And I knew exactly where I had to start.

With Josie locked up, I'd lost access to my most valuable source of local information, but I wasn't completely lacking in options. It was a small town, after all, and there were only so many places a big group coming in from out of town could stay.

The morning after my chili dinner with Calvin, I left for work early so I could swing by the Best Western hotel and see if Leland Price, the manager, was on duty. We were on good terms, if not exactly friends, and he'd helped me out in the past when I needed to speak with someone who was staying there. He might wonder why I needed to talk to Chelsea Haven, but I figured I'd deal with that problem when—and if—the time came.

True, there was always the chance that Chelsea wasn't staying at the Best Western at all, had instead booked one of Globe's small handful of Airbnb vacation rentals, but I didn't think so. For one thing, Josie's friend Mavis owned most of them, and I was pretty sure Josie would have told me if anyone from the Life Springs Church contingent was renting one. Also, since Thanksgiving was now two days away—a fact I couldn't quite allow myself to forget, not when I had a dozen people coming over to the house for a sit-down dinner in forty-eight hours—that meant pretty much all the Airbnbs in town had been rented for weeks, if not months. The church's gig here had been a last-minute operation, and so I guessed they must have had to get rooms at the hotel instead.

And if Chelsea Haven wasn't staying here, then I'd get in touch with Mavis and find out if Chelsea had managed to book one of Mavis's vacation rentals. I knew no one from Life Springs Church had rented out my friend Hazel's place, since she'd already booked it months earlier.

First things first, though.

The parking lot at the Best Western looked more crowded than usual, although I told myself that wasn't so strange, not with Thanks-giving the day after tomorrow and people's families coming to town for a visit. There were a good number of out-of-state plates, too, although I had to believe that the people from Life Springs probably had flown to Arizona and then rented as many cars as they needed at the airport.

To my relief, Leland was working at the front desk when I came in. He was a man of medium height, maybe around ten years older than I, with thinning brown hair and kind brown eyes. As soon as he saw me, he offered a smile.

"Hi, Selena," he said. "If you're looking for a room, I'm afraid we're full up."

Something I'd already guessed from the number of vehicles in the parking lot, but at least his comment confirmed my suspicions. And because I knew he was pulling my leg a little about the room, since it was common knowledge that I lived just a few miles from here, I only returned his smile.

"No, I don't need a room," I replied. "But I was hoping you could tell me if the people from Life Springs Church are staying here."

At once, his expression turned sober, as he appeared to recall their visit hadn't ended very well. "They are," he said. "Or at least, some of them still are. Most of the group left late yesterday—I guess they needed to get back to their headquarters in Texas. Dallas, I think."

Well, that explained the hint of an accent I'd heard in Aaron Galloway's voice. And it also figured that someone in charge of a megachurch would want to live in Texas, where there wasn't any state income tax.

Fighting back my worry that Chelsea Haven might have been one of those who'd already departed, I asked, "Do you know if Ms. Haven is still here?"

To my relief, Leland nodded at once. "Yes, she and her husband stayed behind. I think they're sticking around Globe until the medical examiner releases Pastor Galloway's remains." Now he looked even more somber, and he added, "That was an awful business."

"Yes, it was," I agreed.

"And now you're trying to solve his murder," Leland said simply, as if my doing so was a foregone conclusion. Then again, since I'd already blundered my way through a half dozen previous murder investigations, I supposed he wasn't too out of line for thinking such a thing.

"I'm trying to help my friend," I said, and he nodded.

"Yeah, it's crazy that Henry Lewis would think Josie had anything to do with all this,"

Leland replied. "She put in a good word for me when I applied for this job, so I'll do what I can to return the favor. What do you need?"

This was going better than I'd hoped. I'd been worried that I'd have to cajole Leland into giving me Chelsea Haven's room number, but it sounded as though he was willing to just hand it over. True, doing so wasn't exactly kosher, although I would never divulge exactly where I'd gotten that particular piece of information.

"Can you tell me which room Ms. Haven and her husband are staying in?" I asked.

"Two-twelve," Leland said promptly, without even taking a glance at his computer. Maybe he had a habit of memorizing such things, or maybe that particular bit of information had stuck in his brain because of the tragic circumstances surrounding it.

Either way, I knew I should be glad that I didn't have to take any extraordinary measures to figure out where Ms. Haven had gone to ground.

"And she's here now?" I inquired next. "She and her husband haven't gone out for breakfast or anything like that?"

"Her husband went out about an hour ago and came back with some stuff from Cloud Coffee," Leland told me. "But I didn't notice either of them leaving the hotel after that, so I suppose that means they're still here."

Even better. Not that I expected him to keep tabs on everyone coming and going from the Best Western, but with the way the front office was situated, Leland could definitely see when cars left the parking lot and when they returned.

And if the Havens really were here, then I definitely needed to seize the moment.

"Thank you so much, Leland," I said. "I really appreciate your help—and I know Josie will, too."

"It's the least I could do," he replied. Then he leaned closer to me and said in a conspiratorial undertone, "And I'll make sure Chief Lewis doesn't know anything about this."

Even better. Maybe Leland had decided that I had a better chance of cracking the case than the police chief, and therefore it was important to make sure Henry didn't get in my way.

I shot him a grateful smile and headed out of the office, then made my way to the staircase that led to the second floor. Room 212 was halfway down the corridor that bisected the top half of the building. It had a "Do Not Disturb" sign hanging from the handle, and I frowned. Obviously, the Havens probably wouldn't be too thrilled about my intrusion.

But I didn't work for the hotel, and this was

urgent. They could be as cranky as they wanted…as long as they were willing to answer my questions.

Before I could lose my nerve, I raised a hand and knocked on the door. A long silence followed that knock, so long it made me wonder if they planned to simply ignore me until I went away.

Well, that wasn't going to happen. I might have been an airy-fairy Gemini with both my moon and my ascendant in Libra, but I had just enough Capricorn placements in the outer planets that I could be darn stubborn when the occasion rose. I was willing to wait out here for as long as it took.

However, that didn't mean I wouldn't try to hurry things along.

I knocked again. This time, the door opened a moment later, and a tall man with sandy blond hair and a not entirely convincing spray tan glared out at me.

"What do you want?"

"Mr. Haven?" I said politely, then went on without waiting for a reply, "I'm Selena Marx. I was hoping I could talk to you and your wife for a moment."

"If you're selling something, we're not interested," he snapped.

I reflected that his was sort of an ironic

response, considering the organization his wife worked for made millions off selling their religion. However, since I definitely didn't want to get into an argument with him, I maintained a pleasantly neutral expression and said, "Oh, I'm not selling anything. I just wanted to talk to you about Pastor Galloway."

Right then, Chelsea came up to the door. She looked very different from the self-assured woman who'd talked to Josie and Joyce and me in the park a few days earlier, her eyes now reddened with grief, her blonde hair pulled back into a lank ponytail rather than its former elegant twist.

"You're the woman with the woo-woo shop," she said, pale mouth pulling into a frown. "What do you want?"

Clearly, grief hadn't softened her stance on all things New Age. "I'm trying to help," I replied. "That's all. Can I talk to you for a minute?"

Chelsea hesitated. Her husband looked down at her for a moment, his expression unreadable.

Then he said, "Sure. Come on in."

A shadow moved over his wife's features, and I got the impression she would have liked to protest. However, it appeared she didn't want to make a scene, so she moved aside when he opened the door further, allowing me to enter.

This room looked pretty much like every other one at the Best Western, with its Southwest-themed prints on the wall and institutionally characterless furniture filling the space. I noted how it had two queen beds rather than a single king, but that could have been simply because a king room wasn't available when they checked in.

"Thanks for speaking with me," I said after Chelsea's husband shut the door. "And you are…?"

Now he looked just slightly discomfited, as if he'd belatedly realized he should have offered his own name after I introduced myself. "I'm Robert Haven," he responded, then added, "Chelsea's husband. I'm also the chief accountant for Life Springs Church."

Keeping it in the family, it seemed. I almost wanted to ask a tart question about how the church's check to the city had managed to bounce, then decided that probably wasn't a very good way to open the conversation.

"You're friends with the woman who killed Aaron," Chelsea said next, her tear-reddened eyes narrowing with dislike.

"Josie didn't kill Pastor Galloway," I retorted, although I was trying my hardest to keep my tone level. "I'm trying to find out who really did."

She sniffed, but Robert Haven frowned and said, "I thought Chelsea said you owned a shop here in town. You also work for the police?"

"No," I said. "I guess you could call solving crimes kind of a hobby of mine. You can ask around if you don't believe me."

None of this appeared to sit very well with Chelsea, because she said, her voice hard, "We already talked to your chief of police and told him everything we knew. It's obvious that your friend Josie murdered Aaron—she had a motive and the opportunity."

A motive that would never have existed in the first place if that damn check hadn't bounced. "She might have had the opportunity," I said tartly, "but she certainly wouldn't kill someone over a bad check."

That comment made Robert wince ever so slightly. No doubt he was thinking the incident had given him something of a professional black eye. "I apologize for that," he said stiffly. "I was in the process of moving funds around and didn't realize Chelsea had written a check against that account."

After he spoke, he sent the briefest sideways glance in his wife's direction, one that came and went almost in the blink of an eye. However, I'd picked up something in that one crucial second.

He was angry with her. Very, very angry.

Maybe over the check…or maybe not. There was definitely something else going on here, something that didn't have anything to do with Aaron Galloway's murder or even that bounced check. No, it was something I gleaned from their body language, how they seemed to be all crossed arms and gazes that wouldn't quite meet.

I desperately wanted all those little tells to mean something, even though I wasn't sure whether they really did.

And it seemed significant to me that both the beds were rumpled and appeared to have been slept in, which felt odd to me. There'd been a goof-up at one of the B&Bs Calvin and I had stayed in during our honeymoon, and we'd been given two queen beds instead of the king we'd requested. We'd made the best of it, snuggling in the cramped quarters, but there hadn't been even the slightest question that we'd sleep apart.

In the case of the Havens, this could mean absolutely nothing at all. Maybe one of them was a terrible snorer, or maybe they'd gotten to a stage in their relationship where they were no longer intimate, although that scenario seemed a little strange for a couple who appeared to be in their late thirties or early forties at most. Still, I didn't know them or anything about their lives, and quite possibly the arrangement suited the two of them just fine.

"It's okay," I said, and hoped it actually was. Chelsea had said she was going to fix the situation with the check…but that had been before someone poisoned Aaron Galloway. She could have completely forgotten about her promise to Josie to get her a cashier's check. "I just wanted to ask if you noticed anything strange backstage at the revival on Sunday, or even before that."

"Nothing strange at all," Chelsea said, still not making eye contact with either me or her husband. "It was all going like clockwork, despite having to relocate the event to Globe at the last minute."

"No one who shouldn't have been there?"

She shook her head, but it was Robert who answered my question.

"Nothing like that," he said. "To be fair, we have a lot of people coming and going at these things, so it's pretty much impossible to keep tabs on everyone. But, just like we told Chief Lewis, we didn't see anything that roused our suspicions. I think you just have to accept the fact that your friend is guilty."

He seemed almost sad while he said those words, as if he understood how I didn't want to admit that someone dear to me could be capable of such a heinous act. His attitude made me like him a little more, but I still was nowhere close to admitting defeat.

"I know Josie is innocent," I said stoutly. "And I'm going to prove it."

Chelsea's lip curled in something close to but not quite a sneer. "Sure you are," she snapped.

Robert sent me an apologetic look. "My wife isn't quite herself right now," he said. "The shock of the whole thing, you know. I wish we had something more we could tell you about what happened on Sunday morning, but there isn't anything to tell."

For just a moment, I thought about pressing my case. However, the angry light in Chelsea's eyes and the weariness in her husband's expression told me any further protests would only be met with annoyance...or worse.

"That's all right," I replied. "I was just trying to follow up on any possible leads that might be out there. If you think of something, though, you can call me at the shop." I paused there to reach inside my purse and pull out one of the business cards I always carried with me. Giving it to Chelsea didn't seem like a very good idea, so I instead handed it to Robert.

To my relief, he took the card from me, glanced briefly at the logo of the moon, and then got out a wallet from a pocket in his khakis and slipped the card inside. "I can't think of anything at the moment, but I'll let you know."

Figuring I'd better end the convo on at least a slightly positive note, I said, "Thanks so much. I'll just let myself out."

Robert tilted his head at me while Chelsea continued to send that narrow-eyed stare in my direction. I managed a very limp smile at the couple before hurrying to the door and slipping into the corridor outside.

Once there, I released a relieved breath. I didn't know what was going on between the two of them, but it was pretty clear to me that some very muddy undercurrents ran through their relationship.

What that meant, I didn't know for sure.

All I did know was that, once again, I didn't seem to have a whole heck of a lot to show for my efforts.

I let out a sigh, then headed down the stairs to the parking lot.

Time to get to work.

10

Skirt Chasing

MY SIDE TRIP AT THE BEST WESTERN HADN'T taken very long, so I got to the shop about twenty minutes before we were due to open. Sometimes Archie would be there before me, but today he hadn't shown up yet.

Just as well. I was feeling more off-balance after my visit with the Havens than I probably had any right to be, and I knew I needed some downtime before Archie made his appearance. Yes, he'd become a lot less prickly after turning back into a man—and entering into a relationship with Victoria Parrish—but he still had an uncanny knack for saying exactly the right thing to get my hackles up.

Good thing I loved him like the brother I'd never had.

We'd moved the shop's safe out of the apartment and down to the storeroom, mostly so I wouldn't have to disturb Archie if I got in early to work and wanted to stock the cash register. I entered the combination and took the little bag of small bills and coins over to the counter and started slipping the various denominations into their designated spots in the register. This was the sort of task I'd memorized a long time ago, and so I could let my thoughts wander while I worked.

What exactly was going on with the Havens? Had I interrupted them in the middle of an argument?

That didn't feel right. The energy between them was super-jangly, but it felt more as though the tension sprang from something farther back in the past than a recent squabble.

What, then?

I pulled out my phone and glanced at the time. Nine fifty-one. Archie would probably be coming downstairs at any minute, which meant I didn't have a lot of time.

Time for what?

Getting some answers.

A quick rummage in my purse produced the little garnet pendulum I carried with me all the time. It wasn't my favorite—that honor remained with the fluorite piece that had a place of honor on my altar—but it would have to do.

Divination mats lay on a display table nearby the register, and I snagged one of them—the pretty piece with a luna moth printed in the middle and the various answers written around it—and laid it down on the counter.

Yes and no answers worked best when you were trying to do a quick pendulum scry, so I fixed a single question in my mind.

Are Chelsea and Robert Haven having marital problems?

The pendulum swung back and forth, then slowed, coming to a definite stop on a single word.

Yes.

Maybe it wasn't something that required a pendulum to figure out, but I had to start somewhere.

The follow-up question flowed naturally from the first one.

Are their problems connected to Life Springs Church?

Once again, the pendulum etched a few graceful arcs above the divining board before stopping on "yes."

Interesting. Was it only that they weren't the kind of couple who did well spending the majority of their time together, or was there something else going on here?

"What on earth are you doing?"

I looked up from the pendulum in my hand to see Archie standing a few feet away, arms crossed and eyebrows slightly raised. As usual, he was nattily dressed, this time in a dark blue cashmere sweater over a maroon and white striped shirt, his brown lace-ups polished to an almost blinding shine.

"Archie, you've worked here long enough that you know exactly what I'm doing," I returned.

"Trying to find the pastor's murderer?"

"You got it." I glanced down at the pendulum, then back at Archie. "Could you handle opening up today? I think I might be on to something here."

Once again, his eyebrows lifted, but he didn't say anything, just let out a long-suffering breath and came behind the counter so he could fetch the key to unlock the shop's front door. While he was busy with that task, I returned my focus to the pendulum and the divining board. It was entirely possible that Archie's arrival on the scene had disrupted the flow of energy that seemed to be giving me the answers I needed, but I knew I needed to try.

Are Robert and Chelsea Haven having marital issues because of Aaron Galloway?

The pendulum swung fast this time, flying from side to side with so much energy, I had to tighten my grip so it wouldn't go sailing right out of my hand and halfway across the shop. When it slowed down, though, it once again came to a stop in the exact same place it had the previous two times.

Yes.

A flash of triumph shot through me. All I had to go on was what the pendulum had just revealed, but I could tell it was giving me the correct answers. These pieces of the puzzle could only mean one thing.

Chelsea Haven and Aaron Galloway had been having an affair.

And that sounded like a pretty good motive for murder to me, much better than a single bounced check.

"A-ha!" I exclaimed, and Archie once again waggled an eyebrow at me as he came back over to the counter and secured the front door key in its special compartment in the cash register.

"'A-ha' what?"

"I think I'm on to something," I said. I paused to glance at the door, but it appeared no one was in a huge rush to go shopping for scented candles or Tarot decks on that brisk November morning. "I think Chelsea Haven's husband is the real murderer."

Because he'd been at the park with me when

I first met Chelsea, at least Archie didn't have to ask who she was. "Why would you think that?"

As quickly as I could, I described the obvious tension I'd observed between the couple when I visited them at the Best Western, and then explained what the pendulum had just told me.

"It makes perfect sense," I said. "Robert Haven must have found out about his wife's infidelity, but he lashed out at Aaron Galloway rather than at Chelsea. And with Josie charged with the crime, he can just stand back and let an innocent woman take the fall for his misdeeds."

"You got all that from a pendulum?" Archie inquired, his expression now vaguely amused.

"Yes," I said severely. "Pendulums can be very accurate as long as you keep yourself firmly focused on the questions you're asking and don't try to get too fancy."

It was quite possible that the Archie he'd been seventy years ago—or even the cat he was up until six months before now—would've found plenty to disbelieve in my comment. However, after living with me for more than a year and seeing me use the various tools of the trade...pendulums, Tarot cards, and my crystal ball...to help solve the various crimes that had disrupted my peaceful exis-tence in Globe, he now knew there was plenty more in heaven and earth than he'd ever imagined.

"That may be true," he replied. "The problem is, you don't have any solid evidence to prove that Robert Haven is the real killer."

My triumph of a moment earlier evaporated as quickly as it had come. While I didn't appreciate Archie being a killjoy, I knew he was only telling me the truth. If I went to Henry Lewis and told him that I knew Robert Haven had murdered Aaron Galloway because his wife was having an affair with the pastor, he'd laugh me straight out of the police station.

Well, right after he read me the riot act about getting involved in yet another murder investigation when I shouldn't.

"Then I'll find some proof," I said. Yes, I'd already shipped off my soil samples to a lab Calvin had suggested—all the while hoping I wouldn't have to wait the supposed six weeks the company's website mentioned when I read the fine print—but maybe, as my husband had said, this whole thing might be much more about the "why" of Aaron Galloway's death than the "how."

The bells on the shop door jingled as it opened, and in came Lynda Holt, probably looking for some scented candles to liven up her Thanksgiving celebration. Her arrival put an end to Archie's and my conversation, but I hadn't forgotten the vow I'd just made.

Robert Haven had to be the killer. Now I just had to figure out how to prove his guilt to the world.

Business on that Tuesday was a little brisker than I'd expected, although Archie and I mostly sold candles and incense, and not many of the shop's more esoteric offerings. Still, I felt a bit more cheerful as the end of the day came around, maybe because we'd made a tidier profit than I'd thought we would...or maybe because I knew we were going to close early the next day so I'd have enough time to pick up any last-minute bibs and bobs for Thanksgiving dinner before I headed home.

And I knew I had my culprit, even if I didn't have any concrete way of showing that Robert Haven must have slipped that poison into Aaron Galloway's coffee. Those were details I was confident I would work out soon enough...or at least, I felt fairly certain the universe would point me in the right direction, even if I didn't have much to go on at the moment.

At about five minutes before five, right as I

was thinking about closing for the day, the bells on the shop door jingled, and Robert Haven walked in. His eyes locked on me immediately, and then he gave a quick glance at Archie, who was over by the bookcase, tidying up a few mis-shelved volumes.

Redirecting his attention to me, Robert said, "Can I speak with you for a moment?"

"Um, sure," I managed. I had no idea why he was here, but I could tell he wanted to talk in private. I looked over at Archie and said, "Archie, I can close up by myself."

His lips parted as though he wanted to offer a protest, but he must have seen from my expression that this was important, because after a brief hesitation, he nodded and headed toward the back of the shop. As he went, he sent Robert Haven a warning glance, as if to let him know he'd be right upstairs and would be able to tell if he attempted anything funny.

I wasn't worried, though. Whatever his reason for coming to see me, I didn't think Robert meant me any harm. My ability to see people's auras came and went on its own, or else I'd summon it every time I needed to know what was going on in someone's head, but his aura flickered into being just long enough—dark blue shot through with little flickers of yellow, like tiny lightning bolts—to tell me that, while he was troubled, there was nothing murderous in his intentions.

I supposed that was a good thing. On the other hand, if his aura had been glimmering blood-red, that would have been the piece of evidence I needed to prove he had no trouble resorting to violence if he thought the situation warranted it.

Once we were alone, I said, "What can I help you with?"

"You're psychic, right?" he replied, his tone almost rough, as if he hated to ask the question but knew it was necessary.

I nodded. "Where'd you hear that?"

"I Googled you," he said. "It sounds like you do a lot of crime solving in your spare time."

"Here and there," I said modestly. "It's not something I sought out...this whole sleuthing thing sort of fell in my lap."

"Good," Robert responded. "Because I need your help."

Although his tone was serious, I couldn't quite keep the corners of my mouth from quirking as I said, "You want me to solve a crime?"

"Yes," he said. "I want you to solve Aaron Galloway's murder."

For a second or two, I could only stare back

at him in surprise. Then I found my voice. "When I talked to you at the hotel, you made it sound as if you pretty much believed Josie was guilty. What changed your mind?"

Robert's mouth tightened. "Nothing changed. I was saying all that in front of my wife because it's what she believes and I didn't want to get into it with her."

Fair enough. Still....

"Why do you care about finding the real murderer?" I asked next.

"Because sooner or later, that thick-headed police chief of yours is going to figure out your friend isn't the killer," Robert replied. "And if he starts digging too deep, he's probably going to discover that my wife was having an affair with Aaron Galloway."

A flush of triumph went through me at this confirmation of my suspicions, but I did my best to maintain a neutral expression.

"Thus giving you a much stronger motive for killing him than a single bounced check," I said slowly.

Robert nodded. "Exactly. I didn't kill the man...although I was angry enough when I found out about the affair that I might have. But 'thou shalt not kill,' and so I restrained my anger. Chelsea tried to make it all her fault, but I knew better than that. Aaron Galloway was a very charismatic man, and they spent a lot of time together."

"What about the pastor's wife?" I inquired, thinking for the first time that it was a little strange she hadn't rushed to Globe as soon as she got news of her husband's death. The only reason I knew Aaron Galloway was married at all was that I'd seen that tidbit on his Wikipedia page, but still.

Robert made a dismissive motion with one hand. "Marilyn? She and Aaron have been estranged for more than a year, although they've done their best to keep their troubles quiet. Can't have the faithful thinking their leader is anything but a paragon of matrimonial bliss."

His tone was so ironic, I had to lift an eyebrow. "You don't sound like a true believer."

He gave a hollow chuckle. "Hardly. Chelsea dragged me into the whole Life Springs Church thing about five years ago, but since it was a good-paying gig, I wasn't going to argue. And it was fine for a while...until I started to have suspicions about Aaron and my wife. I finally confronted her a few weeks ago, right as we were having to deal with moving the revival here to Globe. She denied it at first, but then she broke down and confessed that they've been having an affair for almost a year."

Ouch. Well, this revelation definitely

explained the anger I'd sensed in Robert back at the hotel, the tension between husband and wife so thick, it felt like an overstretched rubber band about to break.

"And so now you're worried that suspicion will fall on you if the truth comes out," I said slowly, and Robert gave a grim nod.

"Exactly. I don't know who killed Aaron, but it wasn't me."

"And it wasn't Josie," I said, and released a breath. "Which means I have absolutely no idea who could have done it." I hesitated, then figured I might as well ask the question, since Robert was the church's chief accountant. "So... what was the deal with that bounced check, anyway?"

He made an odd movement with his mouth, halfway between a grimace and a lopsided smile. "That was me being petty. I moved some money around so the check would bounce and give Chelsea a black eye. I guess I was hoping it might cause some friction between her and Aaron."

Yes, that was being petty, especially when Robert's little hatchet job dragged poor Josie and the town of Globe itself into the Havens' marital struggles. "Did it?"

"No," he said. "I made sure to mention the snafu to Aaron, but he only shrugged it off and said the Lord would sort it out, and that he—Aaron, not God—had other things on his mind right then, like writing his sermons for the event."

Yes, that particular plan definitely hadn't turned out the way Aaron Galloway had intended. I had a few sharp words I would have liked to offer on the subject of Robert Haven's pettiness and how it had caused Josie a world of trouble, but I managed to hold my tongue. I didn't know for sure whether he really would be able to offer much insight as to possible culprits, and yet I had to believe he could provide me with some much-needed information about the inner workings of the Life Springs operation. Alienating him by getting all judge-y certainly wouldn't help me with my end goal of getting my friend out of jail and the real killer behind bars.

"Okay, then," I said, after making myself take a calming breath. "Do you think the pastor's wife knew anything about his affair with Chelsea?"

"Oh, probably," Robert replied. "There isn't much that gets past Marilyn. But after having the man cheat on her for the past fifteen years or so, she would have just brushed it aside. Chelsea was only the last in a long list of women he'd been chasing. I think that's part of what made me so angry—my wife knew her idol had feet of clay, and she slept with him anyway."

I assumed the "feet of clay" comment was some sort of Biblical reference, but since I could count the Bible quotes I actually knew on the thumb of one hand, I just let it slide. "Were the other women the pastor was involved with also members of the organization?"

"They didn't work for him, if that's what you mean," Robert said. He paused there as someone walked past the shop window, but because I'd locked up the place after he came inside, there wasn't much chance of us being overheard or interrupted.

Well, unless Archie was lurking on the landing, listening to every word. I wouldn't put it past him—not because he thought eavesdropping was an acceptable pastime, but because he might have been feeling a little hinky about leaving me alone in the shop with a strange man.

"But they were all members of the congregation," Robert went on. "He was more discreet about those affairs—he definitely didn't want word to get out, for obvious reasons, and the women themselves had plenty of reasons to stay quiet as well—but the rumors were always there. I suppose that's why I tried to fool myself about him and Chelsea for so long. Part of my brain just didn't want to believe either one of them would be that stupid."

"Apparently, they were," I returned. "Do you think that Pastor Galloway hooking up with Chelsea was the last straw for Marilyn, though? Maybe she did her best to brush it off when it was only women from the congregation, but when it was someone her husband worked with every day, she just sort of…snapped."

Robert was silent for a moment, clearly pondering my words, but then he shook his head. "I don't think so," he said. "I mean, anything's possible, but it was definitely in Marilyn's best interests to maintain the status quo. She gets to live in their big house just outside Dallas and has access to as much money as she needs. Aaron pretends to live there, but those of us in the church's inner circle all know he actually lives in a condo downtown. Killing Aaron would get rid of her meal ticket."

A pretty cold way to look at the situation, but I could already tell that Robert was one of those people who was definitely ruled by his head, not by his heart. "You mean this all ends now that he's gone?" I asked, waving my hand in the general direction of Memorial Park, where Aaron Galloway had delivered what would be his final sermon. "He doesn't have anyone to carry on his work?"

Once again, Robert made one of those lopsided, grimace-y smiles. "Churches like Life Springs are cults of personality," he told me. "With Aaron gone, it's probably all going to collapse in the next six months, if not sooner. He and Marilyn have twin daughters, but they've done what they could to distance themselves from their father and his church. They're both at school at Columbia right now."

Yes, New York City was definitely a long way from Dallas. If what Robert was saying was correct—and I had no reason to think it wasn't, not when his aura had flickered into being once again, still dark blue but without those jagged little yellow bolts of anxiety. He might not have won a "Person of the Year" award from me, but I could instinctively sense he was telling the truth.

"Will his daughters be okay?" I asked.

"Emotionally, or financially?"

"Both."

Robert reached up to scratch the back of his head. "I think so," he said after a pause. "Emotionally…well, it's always hard to lose a parent, even one you're not close to. But even though Aaron was running around on his wife and not exactly someone you'd call a model father, he made sure they'd all be taken care of if anything happened to him. There's one trust for the girls with multiple millions of dollars in it, and another for Marilyn, again with millions. I'm not saying there's enough that they can afford to go out and buy a yacht for each day of the week, but they'll definitely be comfortable for the rest of their lives as long as they don't go crazy."

That information reassured me a little, but my brain kept ticking away at the problem. Marilyn definitely had a motive, but it seemed clear to me that she'd been keeping her distance from her husband and was nowhere near Globe at the time of his death. His daughters' connection to the whole messy situation was a lot murkier, though. I supposed it was remotely possible they'd been embarrassed by their father's philandering and wanted him dead so he couldn't hurt their mother anymore, and yet my instincts told me that wasn't the right answer, either.

Still, just because Marilyn hadn't been loitering around backstage didn't mean she might not have had a hand in her husband's death.

"Did Marilyn have any close friends who worked in the Life Springs organization, someone who might have felt protective of her and either helped her carry out Aaron's poisoning, or who might have done something like that preemptively as some kind of twisted support?"

Robert just blinked at me. "That's kind of a crazy theory," he said.

"Maybe," I said calmly. "But I've seen people commit murder for all kinds of reasons —money, revenge, whatever. If Marilyn has someone who feels protective of her, they might have been motivated to get Aaron out of the picture before he hurt her any more than he already had."

For a moment or two, Robert was quiet, seeming to turn the possibility over in his mind. Then he shook his head. "No, Marilyn was pretty active in the church before they had Bethany and Bettina," he replied. "But afterward, she pulled back and focused on being a mother. She told everyone that it was her calling to raise her daughters to the best of her ability, just as it was Aaron's calling to spread the gospel of the Lord."

A gospel he clearly had felt "called" to deliver personally to some of the women in his congregation. That thought led me to another, something I wasn't sure I wanted to voice aloud. After all, this was wading into some pretty murky territory.

But if I didn't explore every possibility, then I wouldn't be helping Josie to the best of my ability. I'd never be able to forgive myself if I neglected even the most outlandish of prospects.

"Do you know if Aaron has any children with any of the women he was fooling around with?"

"No, he doesn't," Robert said firmly.

"You seem pretty sure," I replied, wondering if his assurance was for real or something he was putting on in order to cover up an even bigger scandal than his boss's cheating ways.

Robert sent me a thin smile, then said, "I handle the books, remember? If Aaron had been paying someone child support, I would have known about it."

Oh, right. I supposed that Robert Haven had a better idea than most people what his boss would have been doing with the enormous sums of money that poured into Life Springs Church. On the other hand....

"He could have been paying them out of one of his own private accounts, though," I said. "That's not necessarily anything you would have seen or known about."

Once again, he went silent for a moment. "I suppose it's remotely possible," he responded. "But Aaron was the sort of person who wanted the church to pay for everything. The church owned his house and his cars and his private plane. There wasn't a lot he kept off the books."

"'Private plane'?" I returned, knowing my lip curled as I repeated the phrase.

"Spreading God's word requires a lot of frequent flyer miles," Robert said, his own mouth quirking as well.

And apparently God didn't want Pastor Galloway to fly coach.

While I'd been entertaining the notion that possibly a child from one of those illicit unions might have been hungry for revenge and ready to enact it on their absent biological father, I realized the math didn't really add up. Robert had told me that Aaron hadn't started cheating on his wife until about fifteen years ago, which meant if there had been a child from any of those unions, they would have been fourteen at the most, not really the age at which someone could plan a cold-blooded murder by poisoning. And again, one of those women could be the murderer—the cliché view of such crimes was that poison was a woman's weapon—but I wasn't too sure about that. If Aaron Galloway had somehow been slipping one of his past conquests support payments off the books. then you wouldn't think the woman in question would want to halt the gravy train by killing off the man who'd been sending her money for years.

Or maybe he'd been paying support but had stopped for whatever reason, and that was why he'd been murdered.

Except that Robert Haven seemed pretty adamant about there not being any out-of-wedlock children in the pastor's admittedly seedy past, which meant all the speculating in the world wasn't going to change the situation.

"This whole thing is making my head hurt," I said with a wan smile.

"I know the feeling," Robert replied. "I've been wracking my brains for the past two days, trying to figure out who hated Aaron enough to kill him, and I keep coming up with nothing. Well, except for the part where your police chief would probably think I'm the guilty party if he ever found out about Chelsea and the pastor, but you and I both know that isn't the truth."

"No, you're innocent," I said, then added, "Or at least, innocent of that particular crime."

Robert's head tilted slightly as he sent me an inquisitive look. "Why *do* you believe I'm innocent, anyway?" he said. "I mean, *I* know I am, but I'm pretty much a stranger to you...and I can tell you don't like me very much."

Was it that obvious? My feelings must have betrayed themselves after he confessed to messing up the check for the park rental on purpose, but I still wasn't going to admit to my personal dislike of the man.

"My feelings have nothing to do with it," I responded, knowing I sounded just a bit too prim. "No, it's that I was able to get a flash or two of your aura, and I could tell you're not the guilty party here."

He blinked at me. "My what?"

"Your aura," I repeated. "It's an energy field that surrounds all living beings."

"Like the Force," he suggested, although I could tell from the way his mouth curled that he was joking.

"Not exactly," I said, my tone serious. "You don't use auras like a Jedi uses the Force. It's just something that can give someone who views one clues about your personality and emotional state. Anyway, I can't see them all the time, but they pop up every once in a while. I saw yours when you walked into the store, and it told me you're definitely not the person who killed Aaron Galloway."

"Well, that's something, I suppose," Robert replied. His expression was still faintly amused, though, telling me he didn't completely believe what I was saying. "Any way you could pass that info along to Chief Lewis?"

"Unfortunately, Henry Lewis doesn't believe in auras." *Or much of anything about the special tools I use to find the real killer in a crime we're both investigating,* I added mentally, although I didn't bother to say that to Robert Haven. He already seemed skeptical enough about auras, and if I tried to explain how I also used the Tarot and my pendulum and had a special resource in the spirit of my dead grandmother, he'd probably think I'd gone off the deep end.

Another lift at the corner of his mouth, and Robert said, "That doesn't surprise me too much."

"Anyway," I said, after a surreptitious glance toward the little clock I kept on a shelf behind the sales counter, "I really need to head home. But if you think of anything else that might be helpful, just give me a call." I went over to the counter and picked up one of the Once in a Blue Moon business cards I kept in a pretty bronze holder there, then grabbed a pen and wrote the number for my personal cell on the back. "I'll be here tomorrow, too, but we're closing early because of Thanksgiving."

"Don't remind me," Robert replied, now looking pained. "Neither Chelsea nor I are especially glad about being stuck here in Globe for the holiday, but she's refusing to leave until they release Aaron's body."

Once again, I gave a mental wince. Was Chelsea insisting on staying because she wanted to fly home with his remains, or was it simply because, as the church's chief operating officer, she felt compelled to make sure he made it safely home to Dallas?

Either way, I guessed Robert was less than thrilled about the situation.

Because of that, my tone was gentle as I replied, "I heard they have a nice Thanksgiving dinner option at the restaurant at the Gold Dust casino. You might want to check into that if you know you're going to be here for the holiday."

"I will," he said, although he didn't appear particularly thrilled at the prospect of eating his Thanksgiving meal at a restaurant and not at home. But he also seemed to realize he'd kept me long enough, almost half an hour past the shop's regular closing time, because he added, "And I'll get out of your hair now. I don't think we've missed anything important, but, like you said, if I think of something, I'll call."

A quick nod in farewell, and then he headed toward the front door. I followed him, not because I had something to add to the conversation, but because I wanted to make sure it locked firmly as it shut.

He might have been going back to the cold comfort of a Best Western hotel room and a wife he could no longer trust, but I needed to get home.

11

Twinkle Toes

I WAS ALWAYS GLAD TO GET HOME, BUT THAT evening, I felt especially cheered as I walked through the door and was greeted by Sadie. The little dog was so excited by my arrival—probably because I was running a half-hour late, thanks to my convo with Robert Haven—that she was dancing around on her hind legs, plume of a tail wagging like crazy.

"Sorry I'm late, baby," I said, bending down so I could scratch her behind the ears. "I'll get dinner started now."

Calvin wasn't off work until six, meaning I had some time to fill on my own before he appeared. Normally, I wouldn't have been bothered by having to wait for him to get home, except my talk with Robert had shaken me a little more than I would have liked. He'd been so casual as he talked about Aaron Galloway's numerous affairs, and even seemed more angry than hurt that his own wife had been among the pastor's conquests. I didn't want to normalize behavior like that, and even though I knew I could trust Calvin implicitly, I still wanted him there with me so he could give me a big hug and reassure me that we were nothing like the Havens.

In the meantime, though, I needed to throw together an Asian chicken salad for dinner. We'd both decided to eat light in these last couple of days leading up to Thanksgiving, and I purposely had planned meals that were tasty but not too heavy on the carbs or the calories.

I must have been frowning as I stirred the ingredients for the sesame dressing, though, because Calvin remarked almost as soon as he entered the kitchen, "What's the matter?"

"Oh, the usual," I said, and put down my whisk so I could go over and kiss him on the cheek. "I had a nice long talk with Robert Haven just as I was closing the shop today. He wants me to find Aaron Galloway's killer because he's afraid that otherwise, Henry will suspect him. Turns out Chelsea Haven and the pastor were having a fling behind the scenes."

"Ouch," Calvin said, echoing my sentiments of an hour or so earlier. "Yeah, I can see why he'd have a vested interest in making sure Henry's attentions were directed elsewhere." He paused and sent me a searching look. "Do you think he's guilty?"

"No," I replied as I went back to whisking the dressing. The consistency was almost there, but I needed to make sure it didn't get gluey. "I caught a glimpse of his aura. Whoever killed Aaron Galloway, I'm ninety-five-percent positive it wasn't Robert Haven."

"Only ninety-five percent?" Calvin joked, then came over to the kitchen island so he could place a kiss on my lips—a gentle one, though, since he could probably tell I was currently occupied.

I shot my husband some stink-eye, but because I couldn't help smiling at the same time, it must have been pretty clear that I wasn't really annoyed with him. "It's enough that I think we can take him off the list of possible murderers. We talked for a while and he gave me some interesting insights into the Life Springs organization, but he doesn't have any more idea of who the real murderer is than I do."

"Do you think it could be Chelsea herself?" Calvin asked then, his expression now sobering. "Maybe Galloway told her he was going to break things off."

That particular scenario would have been a convenient answer to my current predicament, but I considered that possibility to be a very long shot. "I don't know," I said. "Robert made it sound as though she confessed everything to him and begged for forgiveness. Also, Josie made it pretty clear that Chelsea was very visible the whole time they were backstage. I don't think she would've had the opportunity to spike Aaron Galloway's coffee even if she'd wanted to."

"Too bad," Calvin observed. He paused for a moment, something in his dark eyes considering, as though he was turning over various scenarios in his head and not liking any of them very much. Sounding very hesitant for him, he added, "You're absolutely sure Robert Haven can't be the killer?"

It was obvious that my husband didn't want to offend me, and that was why he'd hesitated before asking the question. However, I knew Calvin believed in me and my talents, and so there was no way I could take offense.

"Unless my gift for seeing auras has decided to go completely wonky on me, then no," I said. "Believe me, I wouldn't have had any problem believing Robert's the killer…except that all my senses are telling me he isn't. So once again, I'm back to square one."

Now Calvin did smile, and gave my shoulder a reassuring squeeze. "Probably not all the way back. I'd say you're at least on square three or four. You've already ruled out some of the most plausible suspects, so that's got to help."

"Not unless it's enough to convince Henry that he should release Josie," I said, even as I did my best to quell the flood of worry for my friend that rose in me at the thought of her being stuck in a jail cell for the holiday. "She's going to miss Thanksgiving unless I solve this crime before then."

He let out a breath, concern for Josie clearly warring with his own worries that I might be overdoing things. "You're setting a pretty ambitious timeline for yourself, Selena," he said. "I don't think anyone—even Josie—expects you to figure this out before then."

Maybe not, but it seemed absolutely terrible that my friend might be trapped in a jail cell because of a crime she didn't commit and miss one of her favorite holidays at the same time. It just wasn't right.

However, I knew Calvin had a point. Solving crimes took a lot of spare time, and while I had Archie to spell me—no pun intended—at the shop, I still had a ton of things to do here at the house to get ready for Thanksgiving. And although I knew Josie was counting on me, I also knew she would never expect me to abandon my guests in order to chase down some random lead.

"I suppose so," I said slowly, knowing how reluctant I sounded. "But I also can't just put all this aside and have it wait until after Thursday. If something big comes up, then I'll have to pursue it—and I hope you'll understand."

He came over and took both my hands—I'd set down the whisk by then, luckily—and twined his fingers with mine. "Of course I'll understand," he replied, his touch reassuring me just as much as the warmth in his voice. "And I can probably struggle along on my own on Thanksgiving if you're off hunting down some clue or another. Just don't ask me to bake a pie."

"I'd never do that," I said with a grin. Knowing that Calvin understood my position on all this made me feel about a hundred times better than I had a few minutes ago. "I'd just send you off to Walmart to pick up a couple of pies, or maybe a cake."

"No way," he said in tones of convincing horror. "My mother would never let me hear the end of it if I tried to feed her a store-bought pie. She'd be furious with me for not calling her and asking her to make one. You know she's still a little tetchy about not being asked to bring anything for Thanksgiving."

That was true. I'd told Delia several times that I would handle everything and that she only needed to show up and enjoy herself. In my mind, I'd thought it would be a welcome relief for her after hosting huge Thanksgiving get-togethers at her place for the past couple of decades. However, even though my mother-in-law and I got along just fine now, I still didn't completely understand all her thought processes and motivations, and it seemed she wasn't appreciating the day off from hosting the way I'd thought she would and instead was a little on edge about not being able to contribute anything to the feast.

"Well," I said lightly, "if I do bail because I'm chasing down a clue, then you have my permission to call her in as backup."

Calvin let go of my hands and gave me what was almost a sly grin. "Sounds like a plan. I won't even tell her you've been feeding me salad instead of good red meat."

Because our fingers were no longer entwined, I was able to give him a playful smack on the arm. "Don't you dare, Calvin Standingbear. I've got enough on my plate as it is."

He chuckled, then went off to set the table. I

shook my head and went back to the maligned salad, thinking for about the millionth time how lucky I was to have him.

If only all married couples could be as happy as we were.

Archie seemed pretty cheerful when he came into the shop the next morning, no doubt because he knew he would be getting to see Victoria over the long weekend. She hadn't been lucky enough to snag Hazel's Airbnb, but she was planning to stay at the Best Western through Sunday, so the couple would get to share plenty of quality time together. And while a lot of people might have wondered why she wasn't just staying with him, I thought I understood. Yes, it was pretty clear that they had an intimate relationship, but having her spend all whole four days there seemed to be more of a signal than they currently wanted to send.

"Any big plans for the long weekend?" I asked him after I'd sent Kimberly Parker home with several of Joyce Lewis's gorgeous candles. I'd already guessed today would be pretty quiet, since most people were focused on house cleaning and food prep the day before Thanksgiving rather than shopping, but even though it wasn't even noon yet, we'd had more customers than I'd expected, mostly people buying candles. Apparently, they'd decided their homes needed to smell their very best for their holiday guests.

To my surprise, Archie looked almost embarrassed by my question. "Oh, Victoria and I are going to explore a little, and then we're going up to Payson on Saturday night."

"Really?" I inquired, wondering what was in Payson that would draw the couple out in the evening. From what I'd been able to tell, Archie still wasn't entirely comfortable driving at night, and so it sounded as though they mostly stuck closer to home for their evening activities. True, Payson's theater was bigger and fancier than our tiny one just down the street from the shop, but I didn't know whether that would be incentive enough to have them drive all the way up there.

Had the tips of his ears just turned bright red? Like me, he was fair-skinned, and so it wasn't as easy for him to hide his embarrassment as it might have been for someone like Calvin, who was blessed with a naturally darker complexion.

Speaking quickly, as though he hoped his hasty mumble might somehow obfuscate the content of his reply, Archie said, "We're going to a ballroom dance competition."

"Oh, that sounds like fun," I said. His response hadn't caught me quite as off guard as it might have, since I knew from seeing them dance at my wedding that both Archie and Victoria were amazing dancers. "I always thought it would be fun to go watch one of those."

If possible, his ears turned even redder. "We're not watching," he replied, still in that fast undertone. "We're competing."

For a second or two, I could only stare back at him. If he'd just announced that he and Victoria had decided to get married on top of Mount Everest, I couldn't have been more startled.

"You're *competing?*" I said. Before this shocking revelation, I would have stated flatly that Archie Bradshaw was probably the last person I could have imagined making such a public display of himself.

All right. Second to last. I couldn't see Calvin doing anything like that, either, and since Archie was an expert dancer while the man I loved had two left feet on the dance floor, I supposed it was just barely more plausible that Archie might be the one to enter a ballroom dance competition.

Still....

"Yes, we're competing," he said, now

sounding more like the testy cat he'd been not so long ago. "It's just a small regional competition, but Victoria thought it would be good to start with something like that rather than at one of the bigger events in Phoenix."

"So, this was Victoria's idea?" I asked then. That made a little more sense. Not that she had ever uttered one word to me about wanting to compete in a ballroom dance tournament, but she was much better at putting herself out there than Archie was.

"It was *both* our ideas," he said severely, as though he wanted to make sure he disabused me of the notion that Victoria had cajoled him into what seemed like wildly out-of-character behavior to me. "We enjoy dancing together, and we've had several people tell us we should compete. So, we thought we'd try it someplace where the stakes weren't too high."

And the competition not terribly stiff, most likely. I was actually kind of surprised such an event would even be taking place in Payson, which seemed more like an outdoorsy kind of town and not the sort of venue where people would be getting dressed up in spangly outfits to dance the tango, or whatever.

In fact, that mental image made me smile, to which Archie snapped, "You think it's funny, don't you?"

"No, not at all," I said hastily. "I think it's great that you and Victoria are going out and doing things together. Only...." I let the word float on the air for a moment, then decided to throw caution to the wind. "Are you really going to wear one of those sequined jumpsuits, or whatever?"

If Archie had looked pained before, he now appeared like someone suffering the first pangs of a failing appendix. "Not at this competition," he said, his tone stiff. "It's basic ballroom, not Latin."

"Ah," I replied. I had to admit that pretty much everything I knew about competitive ballroom dancing had come from watching *Strictly Ballroom* back when I was in junior high and the movie had aired on one of the local stations in L.A., so maybe I didn't have an accurate picture as to what really went down at these sorts of things. "So...white tie and tails?"

He nodded. "Precisely. I assume you don't have a problem with that?"

"None at all," I said serenely. Actually, I had no doubt at all that Archie would look fabulous in tails. He was tall and broad-shouldered and slim, and one of those men who managed to make even jeans and a polo shirt look like evening wear. An impish impulse compelled me to add, "Maybe Calvin and I should come up to watch. You know, to lend you two some moral support."

As expected, Archie looked positively aghast at that suggestion. "No, I don't think so," he said at once. "That is, it's Victoria's and my first competition. I'd rather not have people in the audience who know us, just in case we flub something."

I thought the chances of the two of them making a major mistake weren't very high, mostly because I had to believe they must have been practicing on the down-low for months before getting up the courage to actually take part in a ballroom dance competition. Where exactly they'd been having those practice sessions, I didn't know, but I supposed they could have been using the second bedroom in the apartment above the shop, the one that had once been my office and had held my altar and bookshelves. As far as I'd been able to tell, Archie had never bothered to put any furniture in there to replace the things I'd moved over to Calvin's house, so the space might have been big enough as long as they didn't try to re-enact the waltz scene from *The King and I*.

"I understand," I said. While I probably would have enjoyed attending the competition, I also realized that Archie and Victoria wanted to go on this first outing by themselves to see how it all shook out. If they ended up triumphing, then they could tell us all about it later and show off their trophies, but if things didn't go as well as they'd hoped, at least they wouldn't have any witnesses to their failure.

Not that I expected them to fail. I'd only seen them dance together at my wedding, some five months in the past, but they'd been pretty spectacular together even then. If they'd been practicing this whole time, then I could only assume they must be thoroughly amazing by now.

And it probably didn't hurt that they were such a striking couple, both of them blond and blue-eyed, although Archie's hair was dark gold while Victoria's was much lighter.

"Good," Archie said, his tone now almost subdued. Maybe he'd been expecting me to put up more of an argument about attending the competition and now wasn't quite sure of the best way to respond.

"But," I added, and was secretly amused to see an expression of faint alarm flit across his handsome features, "if you guys do win this one, then you can expect Calvin and me in front-row seats at your next competition."

Assuming I could convince Calvin to go, of course. I got the feeling that ballroom dance tournaments weren't exactly his cup of tea, but I also guessed that the novelty of getting to watch Archie twirling Victoria around a dance floor while doing his best Fred Astaire impression might be enough that Calvin would agree it was an event not to be missed.

"If you must," Archie said in resigned tones, as if realizing I was going to stand my ground on this one.

I decided not to push things after that, and the rest of our abbreviated day went smoothly enough. After I locked the front door at three, I told Archie I'd see him and Victoria at the house around three o'clock the next afternoon, and then I said goodbye and headed out.

While shopping at Walmart the day before Thanksgiving wasn't terribly high on my list of things I wanted to do with my life, I knew I didn't have much choice. We'd already bought the turkeys, which had been slowly defrosting on the bottom shelf of the refrigerator for the past couple of days, but I needed to get the ingredients for the salad, as well as fresh oranges and coconut for the ambrosia and a bunch of other odds and ends.

When I pulled into the parking lot, I had to take a space near the very back, since the rest of the lot was completely full. That didn't bode well for my shopping expedition, but unfortunately, I didn't have much choice...unless I wanted to waste even more time by driving all the way to Mesa.

A small stroke of luck had one of the kids who gathered up the shopping carts from the lot setting out a fresh batch in front of the store just as I approached the entrance, so at least I didn't have to roam all over the place to scrounge one. It did have a bum wheel, though, one that caught and squeaked every few feet I traveled, and I tried not to sigh. Yes, it was annoying, but at least I'd gotten a cart. Things could be worse.

A sentiment I had to remind myself of multiple times as I tried to thread the cart through the throngs of shoppers who crowded the store, all of whom appeared to be intent on picking up all those little last-minute items, just as I was. However, it seemed the store manage-ment had been on top of things when it came to making sure they were well-stocked to face the onslaught of Thanksgiving preppers, and I was relieved to see they weren't out of any of the items I needed.

Still, getting through the crowded aisles was a real slog, and seemed to take twice as long as I'd planned. It was past four by the time I finally got in line to check out, and another fifteen minutes before I made it up to the cash register.

I didn't recognize the woman working at the register, although the plastic badge she wore told me her name was Nora. It seemed clear to me she wasn't too thrilled to be working that hectic Wednesday afternoon, because her aura flashed into being for just a few seconds as she started scanning the items I'd placed on the belt, murky purple shot through with red, the aura of someone who really wasn't very happy about life.

Well, I could understand why she might feel that way. The Goddess only knew that I'd never have to deal with anything even half this crazy when working at my store, and yet I'd still had days around Christmas when I wondered why I had ever gone into retail in the first place.

And this was just the day before Thanksgiving. I shuddered to think what this Walmart would look like when it opened early the next day for their pre–Black Friday sales.

Hopefully, since the clerk was working today, she wouldn't be expected to come back in tomorrow. I thanked her as she handed over the receipt, but her tone was just a degree or two away from overtly hostile.

Had I done something to offend her?

I didn't think so. No, I was sure she was just exhausted and wanted to get home, where, no doubt, she'd be expected to make a Thanksgiving feast of her own. There had been a wide gold band on the ring finger of her left hand, and so I assumed she must be married.

Anyway, I told myself it wasn't my problem. I'd done my best to be pleasant, and there wasn't much more I could do than that.

For some reason, though, I couldn't quite get her out of my head as I drove home. Maybe it was simply that I wasn't used to people being rude to me. While not everyone in Globe approved of my pagan status, those who weren't on board with a New Age shop being located right downtown just made sure to stay away rather than being overtly hostile.

It's no big deal, I told myself.

I just wished I was more convinced of that fact.

12

Giving Thanks

ONCE I WAS HOME, THOUGH, THE INCIDENT WAS crowded out of my mind by the tasks of unpacking the groceries and letting Sadie outside to her custom dog run so she could take care of business. The day had turned blustery and cold, and I could tell she wasn't up for a walk and much preferred to go out and get back inside with a minimum of fuss.

Which was fine by me. I'd taken care of the shopping, but Calvin wouldn't be home for several more hours, and so I had some time on my hands.

And I realized what I needed to do with it.

"Keep an eye on things for me, okay?" I asked Sadie as I bent down to pat her on the head. I'd given her a treat after she was done outside and also refreshed her water, but she wasn't due to be fed until around six, meaning that I could leave her alone for a while and not have too much to worry about.

The little dog looked more resigned than anything else, as if she knew she didn't have any tricks up her sleeve to keep me at home. She trotted out of the kitchen and climbed into her bed in the living room, then curled up in a very small ball.

I couldn't help feeling just the slightest bit guilty about heading back out when I'd barely been home for fifteen minutes, but, on the other hand, I'd still probably return right around when I'd usually get home from work anyway. It wasn't as though I'd be leaving the dog alone for hours and hours.

Besides, the person I was going to see needed reassurance even more than Sadie did.

Ten minutes later, I was standing in front of the reception desk at the Globe police station. To my relief, Loretta Stillman was sitting there this afternoon, which meant I had a much better chance of success than I might otherwise have had. She came into my shop from time to time to buy a candle or a piece of jewelry, although she steadfastly stayed away from any of the more esoteric items I offered. All the same, I could count on her as an amicable acquaintance, if not an actual friend.

"Hi, Loretta," I said, and the smile of greeting she'd been wearing slipped a little.

"Henry's not here," she replied quickly.

I supposed I could understand why she might have thought I was at the station searching for her boss, since the last time I'd come here on "official" business, it had been to enlist the chief's help in going to apprehend the man who'd killed celebrity TV host Dillon James. This time, however, I had no reason to see Henry. He'd taken his position on Aaron Galloway's murder, and I knew it would require a mountain of evidence to budge him.

Evidence I didn't currently possess.

"That's okay," I said. "I'm here to see Josie."

At once, Loretta's expression grew even more shuttered. "She's not supposed to see anyone except family and her lawyer outside visiting hours."

Not completely surprising, but if Henry wasn't here to stop me....

"Only for a few minutes," I pleaded. "I just wanted to check on her and see how she's holding up." Since Loretta was still looking dubious, I added with a smile, "I promise I didn't bring any nail files with me."

A long hesitation, and then she released a

sigh. "Okay. Five minutes. And if anyone asks, you weren't here."

"Mum's the word," I said, and made a lip-zipping motion near my mouth.

Not that any of this really mattered, because the police station had cameras everywhere, and my visit to Josie would be recorded for posterity. However, I had a feeling no one really checked those recordings unless something out of the ordinary occurred at the station, and I knew I'd do my darnedest to make sure this visit was brief and completely unworthy of note.

Or so I hoped, anyway.

Loretta glanced around, but the station appeared even sleepier than usual on that particular Wednesday before Thanksgiving, with absolutely no one in the waiting area. I had to assume Henry's deputies were out on patrol just as they always were, and other police business must have been taking place in the building's offices, and yet it seemed pretty clear to me that no one was paying too much attention to what their receptionist/deputy was up to.

"Come on," she said, sounding resigned.

Once again, I made my way to the back of the station where the jail cells were located. The police station had four, and currently, Josie's was the only one that was occupied.

She stood up as soon as I approached, a

wide smile wreathing her round face. "Selena!" she exclaimed. "Thanks so much for dropping by!"

Her tone was so cheerful, she sounded as though she was greeting me on her front porch and not in one of Globe's tiny jail cells. Loretta sent me a quick glance, as if to remind me that I didn't have a lot of time, and then hurried off to resume her post at the front desk.

"You sound good, Josie," I said, feeling more relieved than I might have expected, given the situation.

Her hand lifted in one of her usual airy waves. "Oh, well," she said deprecatingly. "I do my best to make the most of a bad situation. To be honest, I'm just horribly bored."

I could see that. Most of the time, she was a whirlwind of nonstop activity, showing houses, photographing new listings, managing her beloved Old Globe Theatre Company…and now presiding over City Council meetings in her new role as mayor. The only time I'd ever seen her completely still was when she'd broken her ankle the summer before and was confined to a wheelchair for a week or so until her orthopedist gave her the go-ahead to graduate to crutches.

"I'm sorry about that," I said. "It must be hard to keep yourself occupied."

She glanced back toward the bed in her cell,

where a paperback book lay on the thin mattress. "I'm trying to catch up on my reading," she told me. "But sometimes it's hard to concentrate."

"Have they had a lot of people in here?" I asked, stepping on my tongue before I could say "other prisoners." The last thing I wanted was to lump my friend in with the usual group of miscreants who generally landed in Globe's jail —people driving drunk, or maybe one of the bikers who got a little too rowdy while drinking their weight in beer at the Drift Inn, the seedy bar at the lower end of Broad Street not too far from my shop.

To my relief, Josie shook her head. "Not really. One night Leon Mackey got to sleep it off in the cell at the end of the row, but that's been it. I suppose everyone's being on their best behavior."

Maybe...or maybe any mischief they'd gotten up to had taken place far from a deputy's watching eyes.

"Do you have any new developments in Pastor Galloway's death?" she asked, a reasonable enough question. I was sure Josie thought that was why I'd dropped in today.

"Not really," I replied. "Or at least, nothing that might help you get out of here. I have a few more people I'm pretty sure I can take off the list of possible suspects, but nothing to tell me who actually did the deed."

Her face fell…but only for a moment. Then she brightened up, light blue eyes taking on their usual twinkle. "Well, I'm sure it's only a matter of time," she assured me. "After all, you've solved every other case that's crossed your path."

Maybe so, but every winning streak had to come to an end at some point. I didn't tell Josie that, of course, because I'd come by here to reassure her I was still working on the case and that she shouldn't give up hope. "I know," I said. "I just wish it would happen a little faster. I hate the idea of you having to spend Thanksgiving in here."

She let out a sigh. "Oh, well," she said, and waved a hand again, although I sensed something half-hearted about the gesture, as though she was doing her best to put on a brave face and not entirely succeeding. "It won't be like going to Thanksgiving dinner, I suppose, but Henry told Brett that he and Terry could put together a plate from their meal and bring it to me here. So at least I'll get to have some of Terry's cooking—including her famous pecan pie—and I can pretend I'm at their house with them."

That piece of news made me feel just the

tiniest bit better. No, it wouldn't be the same as spending the holiday with her family, but she'd get to eat some decent food and not be consigned to Salisbury steak, or whatever else it was the Globe jail's inmates usually got for dinner. Not that Josie had been eating any of that slop anyway, since it sounded as though Brett and Terry had been bringing her takeout from her favorite local restaurants.

"Oh, that's good to hear," I said. "All the same, I'm going to keep chipping away at the case as best I can. Maybe if the fates smile on us all, I'll still be able to figure out who the real killer is before then, and you'll get to have dinner at Brett's house."

For just a second or two, the bright smile Josie was wearing wavered a bit. Her aura flickered into being as well, its usual cheerful turquoise—a shade or two darker than her eyes—shot through with murkier shades of brown and deep maroon, showing her inner uncertainty. Clearly, she wanted to believe me…and wasn't sure she could.

I couldn't blame her for feeling dubious. Mostly, I'd made that comment about solving the crime before Thanksgiving to make her feel better, and not because I had anything concrete to go on. After all, I had less than twenty-four hours before most people would be sitting down to their holiday meals. And since any useful clues were pretty thin on the ground at the moment, I really didn't see how I could possibly come through for her.

She must have picked up on my unease, because she reached over and gave me a reassuring pat on the hand, as though I was the one in jail and she the person visiting me. "Don't you worry about me, Selena," she said stoutly. "I'm just fine in here. To tell the truth, it's probably a good thing that Brett and Terry are bringing me just that one plate of food. If I were at their Thanksgiving dinner in person, I'm sure I'd be having second or third helpings."

And she sent a rueful smile down at her plump form. That orange jumpsuit she was wearing definitely didn't do much to flatter her figure.

I couldn't help smiling a little in return. It definitely didn't seem as though her stay here in the Globe jail had done much to help her trim down—no big surprise, since she seemed to be living on takeout for the duration.

"Well, I'm still going to try my best," I said, and she nodded.

"I know you will," she replied. "But I don't want you to be too hard on yourself if you can't manage to track down Pastor Galloway's murderer before then. And I definitely don't want you to disrupt your Thanksgiving dinner. I'm just fine in here."

That was an outright lie—she might not have slimmed down at all while stuck here in jail, but she also didn't look much like herself, pale and with shadows under her eyes. That thin mattress on the bed definitely didn't look very comfortable, and I had to believe she wasn't getting nearly enough sleep.

But I could tell she didn't want to dwell on those discomforts, or make me feel as though I wasn't doing enough to help her. She might have hated being stuck in jail, but I knew she would hate even more to have kept me from enjoying my first Thanksgiving as part of Calvin's family.

Because I didn't want to linger—the longer I stayed, the more chance someone would realize Josie had a visitor, and figure out that Loretta had let them in to see her—I gave my friend another encouraging smile, then said goodbye before hurrying out to the reception area. As I passed through, I tilted my head slightly at Loretta, hoping she would recognize the gesture of thanks and realize why I hadn't stopped to chat. She inclined her head in return, signaling that she understood why I was hurrying out.

After all, I might have managed to meet

with Josie without anyone noticing, but I also knew when not to press my luck.

———

Calvin and I had a quiet dinner that night and went to bed early, since we knew we had a big day tomorrow. Of course, that didn't stop him from pulling me into his arms after I slipped under the covers and showing to me once again how glad he was that I would always be there next to him. As I began to drift off toward sleep, my head pillowed on his shoulder, I could only hope Josie would also be able to get a few decent hours of slumber that night.

Sadie jumped on the bed the next morning at six-thirty, tail wagging, just as she did every day. Or rather, any day when Calvin didn't have to be up before the crack of dawn for an early shift.

But he had today off, although he had to work on Friday and Saturday. I wasn't completely thrilled about that, because I would have liked to spend more time together over the holiday. However, at least he didn't have a shift on Thanksgiving itself, and I told myself I should get in the spirit of the day and be thankful for that.

Honestly, between doing some last-minute

tidying up and making sure the table was set to perfection and then heading into the kitchen for the real hard work, I didn't have much time to worry about Josie or anything else. If I'd been struck by inspiration, I of course would have dropped everything to pursue any leads that presented themselves, but it seemed my crime-fighting muse also had the day off, because I couldn't think of a darn thing that seemed remotely useful.

Something was tickling at the back of my mind, though, something that told me I'd dropped a thread somewhere, even if I couldn't think of what it might be. If I hadn't been in the middle of prepping a sit-down dinner for a dozen people, I might have gone into my office and tried a Tarot reading, or maybe even called on my Grandma Ellen to give me a hand. Unfortunately, that tiny whisper of a thought wasn't enough to justify leaving everyone in the lurch, and so I soldiered on in the kitchen, murmuring a "sorry" to Josie in my mind as I chopped and stirred and hovered near the oven, watching through the window in the door to make sure my pies came out a perfect golden brown.

And then three o'clock rolled around, and the doorbell rang. Our first guests were Calvin's parents, who I ushered into the house and then asked if they'd like a glass of wine. They both demurred—Delia because she immediately wanted to know if I needed any help in the kitchen, and Raymond because he wanted to head out back and see how Calvin was doing with the turkeys on the smoker.

I told Delia everything was just fine and she didn't need to lift a finger, and so, while she looked as if she might have wanted to argue, she instead went with her husband out to the yard to check on Calvin. Honestly, there wasn't a whole lot they could really do to help, because once food was in a smoker, about all you had to do was throw some extra wood chips in there every once in a while, but I didn't say anything. No, I was just glad I'd be able to continue with my work in the kitchen more or less undisturbed.

Well, except for having to stop every couple of minutes and answer the door, since our dinner guests started coming thick and fast at that point. I exchanged greetings and directed people to the coat rack in the entryway so they could hang up their jackets, but otherwise let everyone know that dinner would be on the table in about fifteen minutes and that there were cheese and crackers on the coffee table in the living room and some white wine in a chiller and glasses in the same spot.

With my guests safely out of the way, I was able to get the rest of the prep done, with the pies cooling on racks on the kitchen counter and all the various side dishes—tossed salad, ambrosia, sweet potatoes, cranberry sauce, mashed potatoes, green bean casserole, and homemade rolls—stowed in their various serving dishes and set out on the dining room table. Just as I was putting down the basket of rolls, Calvin and Raymond came in, Delia right behind them, so they could set one turkey in the place of honor next to Calvin's seat at the head of the table and the other down on the sideboard, ready to be pressed into service after we'd devoured a sufficient amount of the first bird.

The scent of smoked turkey was enough to draw everyone into the dining room, and we all sat down. Because we were having such a big crowd, I'd used place cards to let everyone know where they were supposed to sit in the hope of avoiding any drama.

I didn't hear any grumbling or mutters, telling me no one was too unhappy with the seat they'd been given. Raymond and Delia sat to Calvin's right, while I was on his left, with Archie next to me and Victoria on his other side. The rest of the seats were filled up by Calvin's oldest brother and his wife and children. The youngest of the kids was only four, and I had to hope he would be able to manage okay sitting with all those grown-ups. I'd given him a plastic cup and child-sized utensils, figuring it probably wasn't a good idea to trust him with a real drinking glass.

Once we were all settled and had wine or other beverages of choice filling our glasses— and even little Aidan had gone mostly quiet— Calvin raised his wine goblet, and we all followed suit.

"Let's give thanks for this gathering, and for being able to sit down with so many of our friends and family. Health and good wishes to everyone today, and in the coming years!"

Glasses clinked as everyone murmured, "Hear, hear," or their version of it.

"And thanks to Selena and Calvin for presenting such a feast," Archie chimed in, and once again everyone clinked glasses. Next to him, Victoria smiled, clearly glad that she was having a real Thanksgiving this year. Because she didn't have family in Arizona, and because she was so crazy-busy with her wedding planning business that she didn't have a huge network of friends, she had spent past holidays eating takeout while staying at home in her condo.

No chance of that this year. I had to wonder a little about her taking a whole weekend off for Thanksgiving, since she almost always worked

Saturdays and Sundays, but then again, Archie had told me she was trying to back off from weddings in preparation for launching her career as an interior designer, something she was planning as soon as she finished her certificate course in March.

With the formalities out of the way, we settled down to passing around the side dishes while Calvin carved the first turkey and did his best to make sure everyone received the part they liked best. A friendly silence settled over the table while our guests tucked into their meals...although that silence didn't last long. No, chatter started up soon enough about all different sorts of topics—whether we'd have a wet winter like last year or whether the Southwest's persistent drought conditions would reign this season, Calvin's brother Joe's plans to build a barn on his property, and so on.

However, I noticed that no one mentioned Aaron Galloway's death, or the way poor Josie was currently locked up and awaiting trial for his murder. I didn't know whether Calvin had told his family those were topics to be avoided, or if everyone had decided it was better to keep things light because they didn't want to upset me.

And although Archie sent me a furtive glance from time to time, clearly worried that I might bring up his and Victoria's impending appearance at the regional ballroom dance tournament in Payson, I knew better than to comment on that particular subject. I hadn't even said anything to Calvin, figuring it would be better to wait and see how the competition turned out before I mentioned it.

So we ate and drank and chatted while Sadie made her rounds of the table, trying to see who was the easiest mark. That honor probably went to Victoria, because she'd fallen in love with the little dog and spoke wistfully of getting a dog of her own once her schedule wasn't quite so crazy. However, I noticed everyone did their best to make sure Sadie got some choice morsels while at the same time being sure not to give her too much. And although I couldn't quite keep myself from thinking about Josie and worrying I should have done more to help her out, I also knew deep down that at this point, there just wasn't anything else I could do. For the moment, I seemed to be stymied by a lack of useful clues and even the slightest whisper of inspiration that might guide me to the real killer.

Eventually, we'd demolished all of one turkey and most of the other, and it was time to clear the table and bring out the pies. I'd decided to make pumpkin and cranberry apple, and hoped everyone would have room to fit their dessert somewhere after devouring all that turkey and mashed potatoes and assorted other side dishes.

It seemed my guests had saved just enough space in their overstuffed stomachs to each have a piece, and we lingered over pie and coffee for those who wanted it, or port or just plain water for those who didn't want to worry about caffeine keeping them awake. Once again, the conversation stayed safely away from the subjects of the pastor's death and Josie's unjust incarceration, and after we'd finished dessert and Calvin and I had said goodbye to the last of our guests—Delia and Raymond, of course, who wanted to stay behind and help with the clean-up—I closed the door and let out a relieved breath.

"Well, that's done," I said, and he came over and gave me a quick but heartfelt hug.

"And everything was amazing," he replied. "You're a natural at this whole entertaining thing."

"I don't know about that," I told him. "Or at least, I think it would have all been a lot harder if you hadn't done the turkeys on the smoker. That freed up a lot of kitchen space."

"We make a good team," he agreed, and bent and gave me a savory kiss that tasted of apple cranberry pie and port. "All the same," he added, "I'm thinking it would be awesome if we ordered in pizza on Christmas."

"As if," I scoffed, even though I couldn't help grinning. I had so much to be thankful for this year…but at the moment, I was most thankful that the huge Thanksgiving feast was now in the past. "For one thing," I added, "no one delivers all the way out here."

He gave a grave nod. "True enough. Besides, my mother is adamant about hosting Christmas—she says she wouldn't ask you to have all those kids over here."

And I had to be grateful for that. I loved Calvin's family, but because he was one of five children and all his brothers and sisters had at least three kids each, they did tend to be kind of overwhelming when they all got together. It had been enough to have Joe and his wife Emily over tonight, along with their offspring, while the rest of the siblings and the cousins met up at their sister Rebecca's house. I'd been worried they might feel snubbed at not getting an invitation for Thanksgiving, but Calvin had assured me that they knew we really didn't have room for all those people, and that it was only right for Joe and his family to come over, since he was the oldest.

"Having the whole gang would be a bit much," I admitted.

We were standing in the kitchen, in the middle of gathering up the remains of the meal. The first order of business had been the leftovers —not that there were many of those—but once we'd squeezed the various storage containers into the fridge, it was time to dump the turkey carcasses in the trash.

Not, however, until we'd performed a very important ritual. "We're extra lucky this year," I said. "We have two wishbones to play with."

Calvin grinned, even as he shook his head. "I'd ask you if you really believed in that stuff, but...."

"Of course I do," I told him. "Or at least, I figure it couldn't hurt."

Still smiling, he dutifully picked up one of the wishbones and held it out to me. "Is your wish ready?" he asked.

It was, because I knew the only thing I should be wishing for was the one vital clue that would reveal who'd really killed Aaron Galloway and prove Josie's innocence at the same time. With that intention firmly fixed in my mind, I grabbed hold of one "leg" of the wishbone and pulled.

Only to have the short end come off in my hand. I made a sound of dismay, but Calvin didn't look too discouraged.

"Don't worry," he told me. "You have another chance."

True. I slanted a look up at him and asked, "What did you wish for?"

"You know I can't tell you that," he replied, dark eyes warm with amusement.

Fair enough. This wasn't exactly the same as blowing out candles on a birthday cake, but I could see why he'd want to keep his wish to himself.

"Okay," I said. "Ready for the next one."

He turned toward the platter that held the two birds' carcasses and picked up the second wishbone. Once again, he held it toward me, and once again, I fixed in my mind the image of Josie free from jail, orange jumpsuit a thing of the past.

Then I pulled.

This time, Calvin was left holding the short end. I let out a relieved breath and smiled up at him.

"Much better," I said.

"I'm fine with it," he said amiably. "After all, I already got my wish—and though I won't ask you what yours was, I think I have a pretty good idea."

I shrugged. "Maybe...maybe not. You know I'll never tell."

"Fair enough."

All wishing done, we disposed of the wish-bones along with the rest of the turkey carcasses, then got to work tidying up the rest of the kitchen. The whole time, Sadie hovered nearby, looking hopeful, but once it became obvious that no more morsels were forthcoming, she headed out to the living room so she could curl up in her bed there.

Bed sounded like a great idea, but it was still too early for that, since we'd sat down to eat at a little after three-thirty and it was still only a bit past eight. Instead, Calvin and I settled ourselves on the couch to watch some TV until we decided we'd had adequate time to digest the heavy meal.

Because we were so full, we only held each other after we climbed into bed, content to enjoy one another's presence and nothing more. And even though I was more exhausted than I'd been in a long time, I lay awake for what felt like an hour after my husband's rhythmic breathing told me he was fast asleep, my eyes shut but my mind refusing to quiet down.

I'd had a lovely Thanksgiving...but I'd failed Josie. She hadn't gotten to spend the holiday with loved ones the way I had. No, she was still stuck in a jail cell, with no real end to her tenure there in sight.

Would the wish I'd made be strong enough to free her?

Maybe. All the same, I knew I ccouldn't allow myself to get distracted again. I had to fix this…no matter what.

13

Fractured Friends

It felt way too early to wake up at six-thirty the next morning, but Calvin had to be at work by eight. Yes, he was the chief, and so a few minutes of tardiness probably weren't that big a deal. At the same time, though, I knew he wanted to make a good impression on his deputies and model the sort of behavior he wanted to see from them.

So, I saw him off after making him a breakfast scramble with leftover smoked turkey and jack cheese and green chiles, and then went ahead and got ready for my own day. I hadn't planned to be open the day after Thanksgiving —Black Friday sales weren't really my thing— but I figured I might as well go in. I'd be flying solo, however, because I'd already told Archie he could have the whole weekend off.

Which was fine. I had a feeling that most of Globe's hardcore shoppers would be attending the sale at Walmart, or had even driven to Mesa and Gilbert to take advantage of the day-after sales at the big-box stores there.

That theory proved to be nothing more than the truth, since absolutely no one showed up at the store in the hours between ten and twelve. Honestly, though, I was glad of the peace and quiet. There was something about being in Once in a Blue Moon, surrounded by all those wonderful crystals and scented candles and the other items I'd hand-chosen because they called to me, that made me feel at ease, ready to let my mind open and see what I could find.

Open to what, I wasn't really sure, because I didn't have anything tangible to focus on. The mine seemed to be a dead end, since pretty much anyone could access the arsenic in the tailings they dumped at the county landfill. True, doing so would require the person in question to know you could get arsenic out of mine tailings, but again, anyone with access to the internet would be able to discover that pertinent fact in about thirty seconds or so.

Which left me...where?

With a whole bunch of nothing, especially since it would be weeks before I got the results back from the lab regarding the little baggie of tailing dust I'd sent them.

All right, then. Something had been brushing at the back of my mind as I'd tried to go to sleep the night before, and that meant I needed to let myself be as open to it as possible. Maybe I hadn't been able to puzzle it out yesterday because my brain cells had been clogged with too much tryptophan, or whatever.

Resolved on that course of action, I opened a packet of sandalwood incense cones and got out one of the little flat plates used to hold them. Most of the time, I avoided burning incense in my shop, just because some people had pretty bad allergies when it came to that sort of thing, and I didn't want to alienate sensitive shoppers when they came into the store.

However, that probably wouldn't be a problem today.

I kept an old, half-used Aim-n-Flame from when I'd emptied out my apartment months ago on the shelf under the cash register, and I dug it out now, pushing my way past a couple of pens and old receipt books that I left under there for the times when the power was out or my credit card processing system was down. A quick glance toward the front window told me Globe's historic downtown was still pretty much deserted, so I went ahead and lit the incense cone.

Soon afterward, an aromatic curl of smoke drifted up from the cone, telling me it had caught and so didn't require any further babysitting. However, I didn't move, only stood there and breathed in the scent—not too deeply; going into a coughing fit wouldn't exactly help with my concentration—and let my mind drift, hoping I could pick up the thread of whatever had been bothering me the night before.

For a long while, nothing happened. My thoughts seemed to skitter this way and that, nervous, worried. That worry was entirely on Josie's account, because everything in my own life was going pretty swimmingly at the moment. The Thanksgiving dinner had been a huge success, and I didn't even have to worry about doing the same thing all over again at Christmas, as Calvin's mother was going to play hostess.

But Josie....

Something flickered. Not about my friend, but about Thanksgiving itself, which didn't make much sense, since the holiday was over and done, and everyone had gotten along well. Even Archie hadn't looked too put out by four-year-old Aidan's antics, a forbearance which had definitely surprised me at the time.

Was Archie trying to prove to Victoria that he would actually be a good father?

Six months ago, such a notion would never have even crossed my mind. But that was before he'd fallen hard for her, before the curse that had kept him a cat for more than seventy years had been broken by a love that had surprised him more than anyone else.

Well, whatever Archie's future designs on fatherhood, they weren't my concern at the moment. No, I needed to figure out why Thanksgiving felt so significant to me. No one who'd attended the get-together at Calvin's and my house had a direct connection to Josie — and they definitely had no connection at all to Aaron Galloway — so I didn't think that was it.

My head ached faintly. Too much wine and rich food at dinner the night before, probably. Luckily, I kept several boxes of tea in the makeshift break area I'd set up in a corner of the stockroom, and had a small microwave there as well. Since it didn't look as though I needed to worry about any customers wandering into the shop any time soon, I figured it should be safe enough to slip back there and make myself a cup of Darjeeling.

A quick glance toward the street outside told me it was utterly empty, and so I hurried into the stockroom, poured some water into a cup from one of the gallon containers I kept back there as well, then got out a bag of tea from one of the boxes stacked on the same small table where the microwave sat. There were only a couple of bags left in the box, and I made a mental note to pick up some more the next time I went to Walmart.

Walmart....

Something about the name of the store made me go still, as if that was the clue the universe had been waiting for.

But why? I'd wrestled more than once with my own issues regarding Walmart's business practices but had given in to expediency, since it was literally the only game in town and I just didn't have the free time to drive all the way to Mesa to do my shopping. However, I didn't think my moral qualms were the issue here.

No, something about my shopping trip to Walmart the day before Thanksgiving kept sending off little pings, even if I still couldn't quite figure out why. The store had been crazy-hectic, but I'd managed to escape pretty much unscathed, except for spending about twenty minutes longer there than I would have liked. In fact, the only thing that stood out in my mind was the not quite veiled hostility of the woman who'd rang up my purchases.

And the hazy purple of her aura, shot

through with jagged streaks of red, like bloody lightning. At the time, I'd simply thought she was having a bad day, although the muddy hue of her base aura color also signaled someone whose light had been quenched...someone who might be carrying around a huge load of guilt.

Guilt over murdering Aaron Galloway?

That seemed like a stretch even for me, despite my having made some pretty big leaps of faith in the past when trying to puzzle my way through the solution to a crime. After all, just because someone's aura signaled they were pretty angry at the world didn't mean they were a murderer.

And yet....

Maybe she'd gone to the revival, and maybe she'd somehow managed to slip behind the scenes and put that arsenic in the pastor's coffee. All indications so far were that the backstage area had been fairly chaotic, so I supposed it was possible no one would have noticed her. She was the type of woman most people wouldn't spare a second glance for, of average height and build, maybe in her early fifties, with mid-brown hair that showed obvious signs of gray around her face. I had to believe there were probably plenty of other women in attendance at the revival who matched her same general description...and very possibly, she'd been relying on her nondescript appearance to ensure no one would be able to point her out as a person of interest.

Still, vague feelings and some pretty out-there theorizing weren't quite enough to convince me that I should head over to Walmart and see if the woman was working today. Even if she were, she'd be way too busy dealing with Black Friday shoppers to have a second to spare for the crazy lady from the woo-woo shop.

All right, time to get some outside corroboration.

I rummaged around in my purse, which I now kept under the counter since I no longer had the luxury of storing it upstairs in the apartment. An inner pocket of the bag held my garnet pendulum, and it was the work of a minute to go and grab one of the pendulum mats from the display on a table only a few feet away.

Once again, I looked over at the shop window, but no one was loitering on the sidewalk outside, signaling that the coast was clear for now. Even if someone did walk in, I could always explain that I was trying out one of the store's new divination maps, which should probably sound plausible enough.

The sandalwood incense still burned steadily, and I breathed in again, letting the aromatic fragrance bring me the inner calm I needed to focus on the question…and also to help me recall the name I'd read on the woman's badge.

Nora. That was it. Too bad Walmart didn't provide its employees' last names on those badges as well, but most likely, that would have been giving way too much information to the general public.

But that was okay. For what I was about to do, even knowing her first name would be enough to let my intentions focus on her and her alone.

Did Nora from Walmart kill Aaron Galloway?

I held the garnet pendulum over the divining board and remained as still as possible so none of my own body movements could interfere with the subtle cosmic vibrations that would make the little piece of carved stone swing in the direction of the correct answer.

It moved back and forth, but slowly, as though it wasn't quite sure what it was supposed to do. That indecision troubled me a little, because my own experience had shown that if the answer to a question was clear-cut, the pendulum would sketch out a defined arc and then gradually slow as it settled on the response. Now, though, it seemed almost listless.

Even so, I still made myself stand quietly

and wait. It was entirely possible the pendulum would stop in the no man's land between the responses written out on the divining board, and I'd be left with no answer at all. This didn't happen to me very often, but it definitely wasn't outside the bounds of possibility. If that happened, then I'd need to consult the Tarot and hope it might be a little more helpful.

Then the oddest thing happened. The pendulum gradually slowed to a stop, hovering over "yes." Triumph surged through me—a triumph that was short-lived, because then it moved again and swung over to "no."

What the heck?

That wasn't all, though. After the pendulum stopped on "no," it began to move and then paused on "yes." And went back again while I stared at it in consternation before finally wrapping my fingers around the chunk of garnet so I could return it to my purse.

Never in my life had I seen a pendulum act like that. Yes, its responses were sometimes inconclusive, but to have it go back and forth between two equally definite answers?

I shook my head. What did it mean? That Nora was equally the guilty party...and wasn't?

Kind of like Schrodinger's murderer, I thought, and shook my head.

None of this was making any sense.

I knew one thing, though. I definitely needed to talk to Nora and see if I could get to the bottom of the mystery.

―――――

Because it was so dead at the shop—and getting close to one o'clock—I didn't see much problem with putting up the little "be back at" sign in my window and then heading over to Walmart. As I'd thought, the place was packed with Black Friday shoppers. However, because I was actually able to find a parking space, I surmised that the real crush had happened earlier in the day, and now I might actually be able to get out of here with life and limb intact.

Trying not to look too conspicuous, I made my way past the rows of checkout stands, scanning each of the people working there. This particular Walmart had put in a few self-checkout kiosks, but it was pretty clear that the vast majority of my neighbors preferred to have a real human being assist them.

To my disappointment, I didn't see Nora working at any of the cash registers. Well, I'd thought a few days earlier that she probably wouldn't be working today since she'd had to put in a shift the afternoon before Thanksgiving.

Rather than admit defeat and go back to the

shop, however, I instead headed toward the customer service desk, figuring I could ask someone there whether Nora was here today. But when I approached the cheerful-looking older woman who was manning the desk whether Nora was working, she shook her head.

"Nora Lemmon?" she said, then went on before I could reply, "No, she won't be back in until Monday. She asked for the weekend off. Should I leave her a note letting her know you were asking for her?"

"No, that's all right," I replied hastily. Better not to have her know I was looking for her—and besides, the woman at the customer service desk had let slip Nora's last name, which meant she'd be a lot easier to track down. "I just wanted to say hi if she was here."

Talk about your silly excuses. To my relief, though, the woman seemed to take my comment at face value, because she only smiled and said, "Well, maybe you can catch her next week."

I returned the customer service gal's smile and then got out of there. Once I was back in my Jeep, I got out my phone and did a quick search on "Nora Lemmon Globe Arizona."

Sure enough, her name and address popped up right away. People in my adopted hometown generally weren't too good about internet security and hiding their identities from search engines, so I wasn't all that surprised about how easy it had been to find her.

The address listed in the Google results was in one of Globe's newer neighborhoods, on the east side and about ten minutes from where I currently sat in my Jeep. It would be easy enough to drive over there, see if she was home, and then....

And then what? I asked myself. *Are you going to ask her point-blank whether she murdered Aaron Galloway?*

Put that way, my plan didn't seem like a very good one. Unfortunately, I didn't have many options. There was no way I could go to Henry Lewis with my suspicions, because he'd laugh me right out of his office if I told him a combination of a hunch and my garnet pendulum had told me Nora Lemmon was the culprit. I'd need way more corroborating evidence than that.

Which meant I really needed to go talk to her in person, if only to see whether I could get another peek at her aura and figure out if it had been telling me the truth about her mental state.

Anyway, the sign in my shop's window said I wouldn't be back until two o'clock, which meant I still had plenty of time. And while Calvin might have given me some grief about walking into a lion's den...or a murderer's house… all alone, I told myself I could handle it. Aaron Galloway had been killed by poison, not by being shot point-blank or tackled and throttled, and since I kept myself in shape and probably was at least twenty years younger than Nora Lemmon, if not more, I figured I'd probably do okay if our meeting devolved into any kind of a physical confrontation.

That seemed to settle the matter.

I turned on the engine and recited the address to my Jeep's navigation system, then let it guide me east toward the hillside neighborhood where Nora's house was located. As I pulled up in front of her place, a nice one-story ranch-style home with a neatly manicured front yard, I wondered how she could afford to live in Globe's highest-priced neighborhood. From what I'd been able to tell, cashiers at Walmart didn't exactly bring home the big bucks.

But she'd been wearing a gold band on the fourth finger of her left hand, so I figured she must be married, and she and her husband most likely needed both incomes to maintain their current lifestyle. Anyway, Nora's finances weren't the issue here, only her possible connection to Aaron Galloway's death.

As I got out of the car, I wondered what kind of plausible excuse I could offer for showing up on Nora Lemmon's doorstep like this. I didn't live anywhere around here and didn't know the woman, so it wasn't as though I could claim I was just dropping by for a chat. If I had kids, I could pretend I was here on some sort of fundraising mission for their school, but that wouldn't work, either.

However....

The fundraiser notion gave me another idea, one I hoped wouldn't seem too improbable, considering I wasn't carrying a clipboard and therefore didn't look remotely official. I went up the front walkway and rang the doorbell. A moment later, Nora Lemmon stared out at me, clearly nonplussed.

"Do I know you?" she asked. Today she looked much better than she had when she was working the checkout line the day before Thanksgiving, with her thick hair lying loose on her shoulders and some light makeup enhancing features that now seemed just this side of pretty, with her clear blue eyes and surprisingly elegant nose.

"No," I said, and smiled—not too broad a smile, but just enough to show I was friendly and not wanting to be too intrusive. And even though it seemed as though Josie had already found an attorney, that didn't mean she might not need help paying for their services. "I'm here because I'm raising money for Josie Woodrow's defense fund and was hoping you might like to contribute."

Right as I finished speaking, Nora's aura flared into life again, this time looking murkier than ever, although the bright flashes of red I'd seen against the dull purple last time were now dark yellow.

That wasn't anger…that was guilt.

Guilt over murdering Aaron Galloway?

Hope flared in me, even as I told myself it couldn't be that easy.

"Um…of course," Nora said. "Come on in —I need to go find my checkbook."

To my surprise, she stepped out of the way so I could enter the house. Before I lost my nerve, I came inside and let her lead me into the living room. It was furnished with dark brown leather couches and big wooden pieces of furniture, making the whole room seem heavy and oppressive.

Or maybe that was just my nerves messing with me. I didn't like misrepresenting myself, but I'd needed an excuse to get in here. Also, how should Nora even fill out the check? Would it sound implausible to have her make it payable to Josie, considering the beneficiary of her largesse was currently locked up in jail?

"Go ahead and sit down," Nora said, and

pointed at one of the couches. "I'll be back in just a moment."

She disappeared down the hallway after that, while I allowed myself a few surreptitious glances at my surroundings. Several framed family portraits sat on the oak mantel above the brick fireplace, telling me Nora and her husband had two daughters, both of whom appeared to be college age or maybe even a little older. That probably explained why the house didn't feel as though anyone else was living here at the moment—those daughters were most likely off at school in Phoenix or even farther away.

A few minutes ticked past, and then she reappeared, now looking flustered. "I'm so sorry," she said. "I can't seem to find my check-book. Mark must have hidden it somewhere."

"'Hidden it'?" I repeated, thinking that sounded like an odd comment to make.

A flicker of annoyance—or maybe outright anger—passed over her face. "Oh, he's just particular about the household finances," she told me. "Put me on an allowance and every-thing, even though I have a job. He thinks I spend too much money on frivolous things."

It was on the tip of my tongue to tell Nora that she needed to let her husband know we were now living in the twenty-first century and he shouldn't be treating her that way, but I remained silent. Her private life was her affair, and I shouldn't be butting in.

What was even more confounding than her apparent household dynamics was my complete lack of any certainty about her possible guilt in Pastor Galloway's murder. Yes, there'd been that yellow flicker in her aura when I mentioned Josie's defense fund, but my gut was telling me Nora hadn't killed him. There had to be some other connection.

"I did find this in my desk drawer," she said, and extended a ten-dollar bill to me. "I wish I could give you more, but that's all I have on hand."

"It's fine," I replied hastily. While I hated to take the money from her—I didn't want to leave her with absolutely no cash in the house—I knew it would look strange to refuse it when I'd just said I was here to help Josie.

So I thanked Nora and folded the bill and put it in my purse, then stood. She looked relieved, as though she was worried someone might come by—possibly her controlling husband—and discover me there. Nothing in her interactions with me had signaled that she knew who I was or which business I ran, but maybe she actually did know and wanted me out of the house as quickly as possible.

"Is she going to be okay?" Nora asked as she walked me to the door, and I blinked.

"Is who going to be okay?" I replied.

Her brows drew together slightly. "Josie Woodrow," she said patiently. "I still can't quite believe Chief Lewis is keeping her locked up like this."

Oh, right. That's why I was supposedly here, after all. And while some might point out that Nora Lemmon would have a unique way of knowing whether Josie was innocent if it turned out the woman standing next to me was the real murderer, I didn't think that was the case. Something strange was going on here, but I didn't think Nora was a killer any more than I was.

I said goodbye and headed down the front walk to my car, then got in and pointed the Jeep back toward downtown.

Maybe I'd learned something from this little visit...but I was darned if I knew what.

14

Mining for Secrets

ALL THE WAY BACK TO THE SHOP, MY BRAIN kept picking at my conversation with Nora Lemmon. There'd definitely been a strange undercurrent to our interactions, something that put me on edge, even if I couldn't identify what it might be.

And I still couldn't figure out why the pendulum had told me she was guilty and not guilty at the same time.

About the only thing I'd learned was that her husband—Mark—seemed like a real piece of work.

To my surprise, there were actually five or six people loitering outside Once in a Blue Moon, obviously waiting for me to return. I unlocked the door, murmuring apologies, and deduced the reason for the crowd when I noticed the tour bus parked just a few yards down from the store. We got tours like this coming through about once a week or so, but I hadn't really expected any today.

But that was fine. My unexpected customers fanned out through the store, inspecting the various wares, and about twenty minutes later, they were back on their way...and my cash register was five hundred dollars plumper than it had been when I opened up after lunch.

That interruption had prevented me from brooding much over my exchange with Nora Lemmon, but once the store was quiet again, I stayed behind the cash register so I could take a minute to try to puzzle it out. She'd seemed genuinely concerned about Josie's predicament, which wouldn't make much sense if Nora really was the killer. One would think she'd be just fine with having another person take the fall for her crime, even if she was doing her best not to gloat.

True, Nora might be the world's greatest actress, but I didn't think so. Otherwise, she would have done a much better job of hiding her emotions while working the checkout line the day before yesterday.

What exactly was going on here?

Why the guilt?

Frowning, I reached under the counter and

pulled out the pad of paper I kept under there for reminding myself of items I needed to restock or writing down customer suggestions for items I might carry. Maybe jotting down what I'd discovered so far wouldn't make any difference, but I thought it couldn't hurt to try and see whether getting it on paper might help to sort out the jumble of seemingly disparate clues I'd collected so far.

First I wrote down "arsenic," and then listed all the bits and pieces I'd learned about how it could be sourced, and how the mine could be a factor...or maybe not. I'd done a little poking around on the internet and read that you could supposedly get arsenic — and other deadly toxins — on the dark web, but I didn't intend to find out for myself, mostly because I didn't even know how a person got on the dark web in the first place.

Anyway, something told me Aaron Galloway had been poisoned with arsenic rather than cyanide or strychnine or any of a number of toxic compounds, mostly because that particular toxin was readily available in our part of the world...if you knew where to look for it. I'd been fairly ignorant on the topic, but I had to believe that anyone who worked for the mine or was even associated with one of its employees would have had access to that handy little fact.

Worked for the mine….

Ross Davison had mentioned a coworker who was irritated with his wife because she donated too much money to televangelists. He hadn't given me a name, but I had a pretty good idea who that person might be.

The same man who'd hidden his wife's checkbook because he thought she couldn't be trusted with it.

Mark Lemmon. Jennifer had mentioned his name days ago when she'd listed the people who worked in the mine's inspection department, but it hadn't resonated with me at the time…mostly because at that point, I'd had no idea what a controlling person he actually was.

Still, I knew I needed to confirm that Mark Lemmon really did work in that department, mostly because Jennifer had said his name in passing and it had barely registered with me.

Since I had both Jennifer's work and cell numbers stored on my phone, it didn't take long for me to make the call. I tried her cell first, just because I realized she must have the day off and therefore was probably in Mesa with her boyfriend.

Her phone rang four times and went to voicemail. Not so surprising if she was out on a date, like at the movies or something. Still, I chafed at the delay, hating the thought of Josie stuck behind bars for yet another day. I'd thought about stopping at the jail on my way to the shop this morning but realized I was already pushing my luck on that front. No one seemed to have caught wind of my illicit visit the day before Thanksgiving, but I might not get away unscathed a second time.

"Hi, Jennifer," I said after the phone beeped, letting me know I could now leave a message. "It's Selena. I wanted to ask you something about the people who work at the mine. Can you give me a call when you have a chance? Thanks!"

I touched my phone's screen to cut the connection, then set it down on the counter. If she really was watching a movie with her boyfriend, it might be hours before she got back to me, but I had to hope her response would arrive sooner than that.

In the meantime, there wasn't much I could do except return to the list of clues I'd begun writing down. Okay, so…if I was zeroing in on Mark Lemmon as a possible suspect, then I needed to put down anything I knew about him.

Or what I could find on the internet.

Which wasn't much. He had a Facebook account, but either he didn't use it much or he kept it locked down to just friends and family so that anything he posted there would be hidden from a casual researcher like me. Absolutely no presence on Instagram or TikTok, which didn't surprise me much. People in his age group generally didn't have much use for TikTok, and I kind of doubted he'd be posting pictures of that morning's avocado toast or whatever on Instagram.

And there were at least twenty Mark Lemmons on Twitter, none of whose profiles seemed to show they were in Arizona at all, let alone our secluded little corner of the state.

I did find something that said he lived at 1922 Prickly Pear Drive, but since I'd already been to the house in person, that particular fact wasn't of much use. A search of the address itself told me they'd bought the place some ten years earlier for a little over $250K and that it was now worth about a hundred grand more. If the same house had been located in Phoenix or one of its suburbs, that same home would probably be at least another hundred thousand dollars more, but real estate was cheaper around here because of the lack of decent employment opportunities and access to amenities.

Even so, I had to wonder why Mark would be angry with his wife for throwing an extra hundred bucks or so at Aaron Galloway's church when it seemed pretty clear to me that the Lemmons were currently sitting on some hefty equity in their home. True, they might have taken out a second mortgage for home improvements or whatever, but even so, the scanty information I currently had on hand seemed to tell me they must be doing okay financially.

My phone rang then, and I hurriedly scooped it up. However, it wasn't Jennifer's number showing on the screen, but Calvin's.

"Oh, hi," I said.

A chuckle came through the speaker. "Don't sound so happy to hear me."

Despite my frustration, I couldn't help grinning. His tone was amused, so he clearly hadn't taken offense at my lackluster greeting.

"Sorry about that," I replied. "I'm waiting for a call from Jennifer Espinoza. I was hoping she could give me some information about one of the men who works at the mine."

Since this wasn't Calvin's and my first rodeo, he didn't bother asking for clarification, but only said, "Possible suspect?"

"Maybe," I said. "He would probably have known about the arsenic in the landfill, or even had access to get it directly out of the smelter. I'm still not sure exactly what's going on, but I'm hoping Jennifer might be able to give me some details to help fill out the picture."

"Got it."

A year earlier, my husband might have made the effort to dissuade me from attempting to solve the crime. Now, though, Calvin would never try to talk me out of following a lead. He might admonish me to be careful—and honestly, I did do my best not to take too many risks, even if it might not have looked that way from the outside—but he would never flat out command me to step away.

He knew better than that.

"How's your day going?" I inquired next, figuring I might as well steer the conversation to something a little safer than my limping murder investigation.

"All right," he said. "Actually, that's why I called. One of my deputies was in a car accident coming back from Phoenix last night, and I'm going to have to stay late to help cover his shift."

"Is he okay?" I asked, worry flaring through me. The San Ramon Apache police force was more like extended family than a regular work-place—not that odd, considering they were all from the same coyote shapeshifter tribe—and so I knew Calvin would be more affected by an injury to one of them than your run-of-the-mill boss might be.

"A little banged up, and he has a sprained wrist, but he'll be okay," Calvin told me. "But he needs to take a day or two off to feel better, so the rest of us are divvying up his hours so no one's schedule is too adversely affected. Anyway, because I'm helping to cover for him, I won't be home for dinner. I assume you'll be able to scrounge something."

That last comment was delivered in an ironic tone, and no wonder. Yes, our guests had done a pretty good job of plowing their way through all the food we'd prepared for our Thanksgiving feast, but there was still a bunch of turkey left over, along with lots of mashed potatoes and other sides, not to mention a quarter of the pumpkin pie.

"I think I'll manage," I said.

He laughed, the sound rich and throaty even through the cell phone's tiny speaker. Just hearing it made a little thrill go through my body, and I couldn't help smiling. Maybe fifty years from now I'd be tired of hearing Calvin's laugh, but I somehow doubted it. I had a feeling he'd still get this reaction from me even when I was on my deathbed.

"That makes me feel better about skipping out on you," he said. "But I'm hoping I won't be home any later than ten."

"I'll wait up," I promised. It would feel like a very long evening, but at least I'd have Sadie to keep me company. I'd find something silly and fluffy to watch on Netflix or one of our other streaming services, something that would help keep me awake but which I knew Calvin would have no interest in seeing.

"See you tonight," he said, and we ended the call there.

Feeling a little deflated, I set down the phone and allowed myself a sigh, even as I resolutely refused to look at the clock on the shelf behind me or at the time on my phone's screen. There was no reason in the world I absolutely had to keep the store open until five, but since I'd already gone out for an extended lunch today, closing early felt like an admission of defeat.

Besides, the longer I stayed here, the less time I'd be alone in the house, waiting for Calvin to come home.

I did my best to keep myself busy, dusting shelves that didn't really need to be dusted, rearranging some of the crystals in the display case. My busyness was rewarded, because just as I was tucking the feather duster under the counter that held the cash register, my phone rang again.

Jennifer Espinoza. Thank the Goddess.

"Hi, Jennifer," I said, trying not to sound too eager...probably too late, considering I'd answered her call on the second ring. "Thanks so much for getting back to me."

"No problem," she replied. In the background, I heard some muffled noises that sounded as though they might be a football game on the TV. And her next words only confirmed my suspicions. "We went out for an early movie, because Jordan wanted to get back in time to watch the Cardinals game."

A game I guessed she wasn't too interested in, since she obviously had decided this was a good time to return my call. Not for the first time, I found myself thanking the Goddess that Calvin had absolutely no interest in football. He liked to hike and fish and do outdoorsy stuff like that, but team sports left him cold.

"What can you tell me about Mark Lemmon?" I asked.

"Mark?" Jennifer repeated, sounding puzzled. "What does he have to do with Aaron Galloway's murder?"

"Maybe nothing," I said. "But something's tickling my spidey-sense, so I thought I might as well do my best to see if you could tell me anything that might help confirm my suspicions. What's his job at the mine?"

A brief pause followed that question, as though Jennifer was wondering why I was asking when she'd already told me about him days earlier. However, she must have decided it wasn't too big a deal, because she replied, "He's one of the inspectors."

"Does he have a key card that would allow him access to the smelter?"

"Yes," she responded immediately. "He's higher up the food chain, so he can get into most places in the mine." Another pause, and she added, "You really think he did it?"

"I don't know," I said. "But it sounds like he had access. Would he have the kind of equipment a person would need to extract pure arsenic from the mine's tailings?"

"I'm not sure about the equipment," she said, now speaking slowly, as if trying to puzzle this all out for herself. "But he'd probably have the know-how—he has a degree in geology and another in chemistry. That would help with extracting the arsenic, wouldn't it?"

One would think so. I'd left college my sophomore year, realizing that a bachelor's degree wouldn't help me much in launching a career as a full-time psychic, so I wouldn't pretend to know what dual degrees in chemistry and geology might do for a person when it came to synthesizing arsenic.

However, I had to believe it couldn't hurt.

"Probably," I said. "What can you tell me about Mark?"

I couldn't see her, but I got the distinct

impression that Jennifer shrugged just then. "Not a lot," she replied. "I mean, I've seen his personnel records, so I know he's been married for twenty-five years and that he and his wife have two daughters, but that's about it. His is a hands-on job, and he's mostly out in the mine and doesn't spend much time in the office."

It probably would have been too much to hope that he and Jennifer were besties or anything, but I still wished she was giving me just a little more to work with. "Any financial trouble that you know of?" I asked, knowing I probably sounded a bit too desperate.

"Nothing I've heard about," she said. "He's a pretty proud guy, so I don't think he'd mention anything even if he and his family were having some kind of difficulty. Definitely no wage garnishments or anything like that. Except...."

"Except what?" I responded, telling myself I shouldn't get too excited. The exception Jennifer was about to explain could very likely amount to nothing at all.

"Except I remember he needed to have something signed by HR showing that his wife would remain on his health insurance even though she was now working full-time."

I'd never heard of such a thing before, but then again, I'd always been self-employed and carried my own insurance. I had no idea what kind of bureaucratic demands a person who had company health insurance might have to deal with.

"So...Nora hasn't been working at Walmart for very long?" I inquired. Even as I asked the question, I thought I probably knew the answer. After all, our encounter the day before Thanksgiving had been the first time I'd ever noticed Nora working there. It was entirely possible that her shift zigged while my schedule zagged, and that was why we hadn't crossed paths before. Still....

"No," Jennifer said, confirming my suspicions. "I think she started about a month and a half ago. Not sure why, either, because she'd always been a stay-at-home mom the entire time Mark was employed here. I just figured they'd decided they wanted some extra income now that both their girls are off at school."

On the surface, that sounded like a plausible enough explanation for why Nora had suddenly started working outside the home after being a housewife her entire married life. Once again, though, my instincts kept telling me something else was going on here.

Had her husband—who obviously held on to the household purse strings with a grip of iron—forced her to go to work? That would go a long way toward explaining her decidedly sour attitude when I'd seen her at the checkout stand at Walmart. For all I knew, she was doing her best to get written up so she would get fired and be able to go back to the life she knew and enjoyed.

Maybe they weren't having real financial troubles at all, and Mark was only doing what he needed to in order to assert his dominance.

Which made him sound like a prize jackass in my book, but I had to admit I didn't have all the facts in hand. But even if he hadn't made Nora go work at the local Walmart, it still seemed odd that he was worried about money after adding a second income to their household.

Then again, college was expensive, especially if your kids were living in a dorm. And having two daughters in school at the same time had to be serious drain on their finances.

"Anything else you can think of?" I asked. Jennifer had already provided a couple of helpful tidbits, but it couldn't hurt to try finding out a bit more about the guy.

"Not really," she said. "He's not super social. Does a good job, never causes trouble."

Unless he was slipping arsenic into a popular televangelist's coffee. Still, that was only a suspicion and nothing I could prove. "Friends?"

It was a long shot, since it sounded as

though Jennifer didn't have much to do with Mark Lemmon that wasn't in an official capacity, but I figured it couldn't hurt to ask.

However, she surprised me by saying, "He's been friends with Jerry Davis since high school. Jerry works here, too."

"In the same department?"

"No," she said. "Jerry's one of our structural engineers. But it sounds like they still hang out on the weekends."

That was definitely some useful information. I didn't know for sure whether Mark was the kind of guy to confide in anyone, even his best friend, but it seemed as though this Jerry was someone I definitely needed to talk to.

"And everyone's off today, right?"

"Mostly," Jennifer said. "There's always some support staff around, even on holidays, but most people got a four-day weekend."

Meaning that Jerry might have gone out of town...or maybe not. My fellow Globe-ites weren't exactly what you could call world travelers.

"Don't suppose you could give me Jerry's address," I ventured.

As I'd thought, Jennifer shot that idea down right away. "Sorry, I just can't," she told me. "That would get me in a lot of trouble. But I suppose I wouldn't be giving state secrets away if I told you that Jerry likes to hang out with some of the other guys from the mine at the horseshoe toss area at Memorial Park. I can't guarantee he'll be there today, obviously, but I suppose it's worth a try."

"That's a huge help," I said, hoping she could hear the gratitude in my voice. "Thanks so much, Jennifer."

"Well, I have to admit I kind of like helping with a murder investigation that has nothing to do with me," she said with a chuckle. "But I should get going—halftime's coming up, and that's the only part of a football game I actually like."

I laughed a little at her comment, and then we said our goodbyes and ended the call. As I was putting my phone back in my purse, I eyeballed the time on the screen. Two minutes after four.

"Close enough," I said aloud, then headed over to the front of the shop and turned around the "open" sign in the window. I doubted anyone else would be in today.

Besides, I had a murderer to catch.

15

Horsing Around

I DIDN'T GET IN MY JEEP TO GO IN SEARCH OF Jerry Davis, though. Since Memorial Park was only a few blocks away, I thought I'd walk. By that point in late November, almost all of the autumn gold had fallen from the local trees, but it was still a lovely day, with deep blue skies overhead and a breeze just brisk enough to make the weather feel like fall without being so cold I needed a real coat instead of just a light leather jacket over my sweater.

As I walked, I tried to figure out what I should say to Jerry...and what I'd do if Mark Lemmon was also there, hanging out with his buddies and playing horseshoes. After all, Jennifer had said the two men often spent time on the weekends together, so it wasn't outside the realm of possibility that Mark might be at the park, effectively blocking me from talking to his friend.

Well, if that happened, then I'd just pretend I was out for a stroll and keep going. At least I'd seen Mark's picture in the living room of the house he shared with Nora, and so I knew I'd be able to recognize him right away.

Figuring out who Jerry was would be a different story, though. I hadn't stopped to try Googling him before I left the shop, and so I was flying completely blind here.

I'd just have to hope my instincts…or the universe…would guide me in the right direction.

As least no one in the park would think it was terribly strange that I might be out for a leisurely stroll on this lovely Friday afternoon. True, I'd closed the shop early, but I could explain that away by claiming "holiday hours" or something along those lines.

Although I'd never had any reason to play horseshoes, I'd been in Memorial Park enough times to know where the little field dedicated to their use was located. The park was mostly one big rectangle, but there was a small extension at one end that made it look like it had a short handle sticking out, and that was where the horseshoe field had been set up.

When I approached—doing my best to look

like someone out enjoying the briskly beautiful day with not a single ulterior motive in sight—I noticed that three men were on the field, two of them watching while the third one, a stout individual who looked like he was probably in his early fifties, stood with a horseshoe in hand, clearly gearing up to make his toss. To my utter relief, neither of the two bystanders was Mark Lemmon, but a couple of individuals who also seemed to be somewhere in their fifties.

Maybe Mark was spending the day with his wife, since she also wouldn't be working today, or maybe he had some other reason to not be lingering at the park this afternoon. Whatever the reason for his absence, I'd take it.

I approached the trio and watched as the man holding the horseshoe leaned forward and threw the U-shaped piece of metal at the pole some three yards away. It hit the pole with a metallic clang and then slid downward, and his two companions nodded in approval.

"Good one, Jerry," the man standing a little closer to me commented. "I guess all that pie you ate for Thanksgiving didn't slow you down."

Jerry grimaced...and then paused as he caught sight of me standing off to one side, observing their activities. He offered me a friendly smile and said, "Did you want to play?"

"Oh, no," I responded immediately. "I don't even know how."

"It's not that hard," the one who'd just been giving Jerry grief about his pie consumption put in. "Jerry'll get you up to speed, won't you, Jerry?"

He nodded, obviously more than happy to let an attractive newcomer enter the game. "Sure, um…?"

The word trailed off as he gave me a questioning look.

"Selena," I supplied, then stepped closer.

"Well, Selena," Jerry said. "My name's Jerry, and this is Chuck and Mitch." They both gave me a cheerful wave, and Jerry went on, "The trick is to get the horseshoe as close to each pole as you can. Grasp the horseshoe here" —he stopped to indicate the wide part, or the bottom of the "U"—"and then toss it toward the pole. We're supposed to play with both"—once again, he paused, this time to point with his free hand toward a second pole placed at least ten or twelve yards away from the first one—"but we don't really do tournament rules here."

"No, we just like throwing things," said the third man, Mitch, who hadn't spoken up before now. He had a long face that reminded me of a droopy hound dog, but there was a cheery light in his blue eyes that belied his lugubrious appearance. "So don't worry about following too many rules."

"But don't step over the line," Chuck warned me, and thrust a finger toward a pale line chalked on the frost-dead grass. "That's an immediate foul."

"Got it," I said, even as I hoped I could come up with a way to end the game early so I might have a chance to speak to Jerry alone. It was great that he was in the park at all, but if I couldn't manage to maneuver things so we could talk in private, my being here wouldn't help very much in the long run.

For now, though, I told myself to concentrate on throwing the horseshoe, which was a lot heavier than it looked. My first attempt landed at least a foot and a half away from the pole, maybe more, and I let out a breath.

"It's fine," Jerry said, obviously wanting to cheer me up. "You should have seen how much Chuck over there stank on his first try."

Speaking of stank—Chuck shot his friend some serious stink-eye but didn't contradict his words, telling me that Jerry's assessment, while maybe not exactly kind, was at least accurate. I pressed my lips together to hold back a grin and then threw the horseshoe Jerry had just handed me.

This time, it landed much closer, less than a foot away from the pole.

"Looks like you're a natural," he observed, and I shook my head.

"No, not really," I told him. "But it was interesting to try. Do you mind if I just watch for a while, though, to try to get the hang of things?"

"Sure," he said easily. If he was at all disappointed that I'd bowed out so quickly, he didn't show it. Maybe he was just pleased I found the whole process interesting enough that I planned to stick around for a while.

I took a few steps back so I'd be out of the way, then stood off to the side as the three men continued with their match. As Jerry had said, it didn't look as though they were playing by any particular rules except the one about not stepping over the line in the grass, and it also didn't seem as if they were keeping score, but I still found it interesting to watch as they tossed the horseshoes and kibitzed and gave each other good-natured grief whenever one of the three made a particularly egregious shot.

After about fifteen minutes or so, Chuck begged off, saying he needed to get home so he could help his wife with dinner, and Mitch also said he needed to be going, too. Jerry didn't seem too put off by this, and only said he'd stay behind so he could pick up the horseshoes and put them away. I offered to help him, and he nodded.

"Sure," he said, and didn't ask for any explanations as to why I felt compelled to linger.

A few minutes later, though, after Mitch and Chuck were long gone and the horseshoe field had been cleared of any signs of their low-key match, Jerry angled a canny glance in my direction.

"You wanted to talk to me about Mark Lemmon, didn't you?" he said.

For a second, I could only blink at him in surprise. Then I managed to find my voice and replied, "Why would you think that?"

He sent me a smile tinged with resignation. "Because you're the gal who solves murders, and you obviously just figured out that Mark might have something to do with what happened to Pastor Galloway."

Once again, I found myself thoroughly gobsmacked. But because this was indeed exactly why I'd come here to hang out with the guys, I nodded. "If you suspected something, why didn't you say anything to Henry Lewis?"

Jerry didn't answer for a moment. His gaze swept the park—including the large open space where Life Springs Church had erected that huge tent only a week before—and he released a breath. "Because I didn't have anything concrete to go on, just a suspicion. I know Nora was pretty heavily into the church and kept sending them money even after Mark put his foot down and told her to stop. In fact, I'm guessing he made her get that job at Walmart because they couldn't afford all her donations."

Wow. I tried to imagine a situation where I'd meekly accept a job I hated just because my husband forced me into it...and failed miserably. I was pretty sure I would have walked out long before the situation got nearly so bad.

But I had to remind myself that I wasn't Nora Lemmon, and I didn't know much of anything about her life or why she'd decided early on to let herself be defined only by the roles she played—wife, mother—and not who she truly was deep down. If she'd come to me for a reading, I probably would have tried my best to guide her to discovering her true self, but as far as I could remember, she'd never even set foot in Once in a Blue Moon, let alone approached me for a reading.

Not that I really read Tarot for people these days. Sometimes I would do it for fun—like the readings I'd performed at Josie's Halloween party a year ago, the one where Danny Ortega had dropped dead unexpectedly in the middle of the festivities—or I'd pull a few cards if someone close to me had a specific request, like the time my friend Hazel had wanted me to consult the cards to let her know whether she should sell the house she was currently renting out as an Airbnb or whether she should hold on to it. That time, the cards had signaled it wasn't yet time for that kind of change, and so she'd decided to keep it as an income property.

"That still doesn't seem like a big enough motive to commit murder," I said, and Jerry gave a tired lift of his shoulders.

"No, it doesn't," he said. "But still…it's been bothering me. I've heard Mark go off more than once about what a fraud Aaron Galloway was, how he only cared about squeezing as much money as possible out of people. He always sounded really angry."

"Angry enough to kill someone?"

Looking unhappy, Jerry only shrugged again. "I don't know for sure. Mark and me, we've been friends a long time, so I know he has a temper. He's fine when everything goes his way, but when it doesn't…." The words trailed off, and he went quiet for a moment. Then he said, "I probably shouldn't be talking about any of this."

"No, you should," I returned, but gently, hoping that by sounding sympathetic but not too pushy, he'd decide it was okay to open up to me. Maybe this wasn't the time to ask, but the uncomfortable question kept tickling at the back of my mind. "Was he ever…abusive? To either Nora or his daughters?"

If possible, Jerry looked even unhappier at those questions. "Nothing I ever saw for sure," he said, his tone dropping to almost a murmur, even though we were the only two souls in the park at the moment and there wasn't anyone around who could have possibly overheard us. "But there were times when I saw Nora wearing a lot more makeup than she normally did—you know, the heavy pancake kind of stuff, like she was trying to hide something. And she would wear long-sleeved shirts in the summer, even though it was way too hot for that kind of thing and the rest of us were sweating our asses off."

Classic signs of an abused woman trying to hide the telltales of her husband's fury. A shiver went through me that had nothing to do with the brisk wind blowing across the park. No wonder Nora had caved in and taken that job at Walmart. She'd probably do anything she could to avoid bearing the brunt of her husband's wrath once again.

And if Mark Lemmon really did carry that sort of unbridled rage within him, taking out his fury and frustration on the unfortunate woman who shared his home, then I didn't think it was too big a stretch of the imagination for him to have vented that anger on the man he thought was responsible for whatever financial difficulties they were currently experiencing.

On the other hand, you'd think someone with a history of striking out physically would have gone after Aaron Galloway with a gun or a knife or maybe even his bare hands. Poison didn't really seem like it would be his cup of tea...or coffee, if you wanted to get technical about it.

Maybe, I allowed. *But poison would be a lot harder to track down, whereas walking up to the pastor and shooting him point-blank would probably involve a lot of witnesses. The arsenic was a quiet way to do the deed.*

"Does Mark have access to the kind of supplies you'd need to extract pure arsenic from mine tailings?" I asked next.

Jerry wouldn't quite meet my gaze, and instead seemed to find something fascinating on the ground where we stood. "I don't know for sure," he responded. "I know he has a lot of scientific equipment in his garage—an oscilloscope, a little chemistry setup, that kind of stuff. He's always tinkering with something. So I guess it's possible."

It sounded more than possible to me,

although I had a feeling Jerry was trying to hedge a little because he didn't want to come right out and say that Mark Lemmon definitely could squeeze some arsenic from mine tailings if he were so inclined. Maybe he'd gotten the raw material from the mine itself, or maybe he'd gone and scrounged it from the dump, but either way, it sure sounded to me as though he had the means to produce the poison.

And apparently the motive as well, if what Jerry had said about his friend's hatred of Aaron Galloway was true.

"Anyway," Jerry went on, after another of those furtive glances around, as though he was worried that Mark might pop up from behind a bush or something, "it's time I got home, too. You're not going to say anything about this to Henry, are you?"

That was pretty much exactly what I wanted to do. Henry Lewis and I had had our differences in the past, and I still couldn't exactly say we were best friends or anything, but he'd believed me when I went to him with my suspicions about who had killed Dillon James as he slept at his rented Airbnb, and I was definitely hoping the police chief would believe me now, or at least realize there was enough evidence to recommend getting a search warrant for Mark Lemmon's garage.

But I could tell that Jerry was beginning to have doubts about spilling his friend's secrets to me, and so I managed a watery smile and said, "No, probably not. There's nothing concrete enough I could tell Chief Lewis without having him laugh me out of his office."

Jerry didn't say "good," but I could tell he was thinking it. Something about his posture relaxed slightly, and his head tilted in the slightest of nods, a gesture he probably didn't even realize he'd made. "Well, I suppose it's best to have some real evidence in hand first. Have a good evening, Selena."

One hand lifted in a half-hearted wave, and then he hurried off across the frost-yellowed grass, apparently intent on a shabby white pickup truck that was the sole vehicle in the park's lot. I stood there and watched him go, wondering whether I could have thought of something more to ask him...and whether he would have even answered those questions.

I let out a breath, and headed back to the shop so I could get my own car.

Time to go home.

———

The house felt very quiet, despite Sadie's frenzied dance of greeting as I walked in the front door. Probably, it was the realization that Calvin wouldn't be home for hours which made me feel as though the place was so empty...or maybe the uncomfortable thought that I was almost sure Mark Lemmon was our murderer but couldn't do much about it, not with my current complete lack of any evidence except a couple of hunches and a few unsettling comments from his supposed best friend.

I wanted to be angry with Jerry for back-tracking on the story he told me, but I thought I understood why he'd started hedging there at the end of our conversation. He might have harbored some suspicions, but the two men had known each other for decades. It must have been hard for him to admit to himself that Mark might be capable of cold-blooded murder, even if he had a history of domestic violence he was doing his best to hide.

If that was what was really going on with the Lemmons at all. There could have been some other explanation for Nora's occasional attempts at heavy-handed makeup or the way she didn't seem to want to bare her arms during hot weather. I remembered that my mother had a friend with lupus, and Renée also covered up all the time because sun exposure could really do a number on her sensitive skin. Maybe that was Nora's reason for wearing long sleeves in the middle of July…or maybe it really was true that she didn't want people to discover her husband was physically abusive.

The sun had almost gone down, but enough light lingered that I could still take Sadie for our usual walk down the driveway and along one side of the dirt road that led to our house. It dead-ended at the property, since our home was the last settled piece of land before the real wilderness began, and I felt safe walking there because no one had any reason to drive all the way out here unless they were specifically coming to see us.

A car was rattling its way down that road now, though, and I frowned. Calvin wasn't due home for hours, and I definitely wasn't expecting any visitors. I squinted through the gloaming as I reached the edge of the driveway, trying to see who it might be. The vehicle wasn't one I recognized, an oversized SUV like a Suburban or a Tahoe, although I couldn't make out the badging. The only thing I could tell was that a man appeared to be driving the thing, someone partly hunched over the steering wheel, as though hanging on to it like that could somehow make the SUV go faster just by sheer force of will.

And then it swerved and came straight at me and Sadie.

I didn't even stop to think. Heart pounding, I scooped up my little dog and bolted down the driveway, running like a madwoman toward the front door. Behind me, a rattle of gravel signaled that the SUV hadn't given up its pursuit but was now plowing along the drive at top speed. And while Sadie didn't usually like to be carried and wanted to prove to both Calvin and me—and the world at large—that she could get along under her own power just fine, she didn't fuss as I clutched her with one hand, using the other to desperately scrabble in my purse for my keys.

There. My frantic, searching fingers found them exactly where they were supposed to be, tucked away in an inner pocket of the bag. I couldn't allow myself the luxury of a sigh of a relief, though, but only yanked them out, even as a final, ominous spray of gravel told me the SUV had come to a stop. A second later, the slam of a car door told me I didn't have much time.

Not daring to look back, I inserted the key in the lock and turned it. At once, the door swung inward, and I took a gasp of a breath and hurried inside. Just as I was about to slam it shut, however, a man's hand grasped the edge and forced it open.

"You and I need to talk," said Mark Lemmon.

16

The Wages of Sin

BECAUSE I KNEW I COULDN'T WIN A DOOR-wrestling match with a man who had at least six inches and fifty pounds on me, I didn't even try. No, instead I bolted for the kitchen, where we had a land line phone affixed to the wall next to the pantry. While we weren't exactly living off grid at the house, it was isolated enough that cell service was spotty and we had to rely on a satellite service for our internet, and that was why we didn't depend solely on our cell phones.

Behind me, I heard heavy footsteps, and realized that Mark Lemmon didn't have any intention of giving up his pursuit. Luckily, though, I knew the house and he didn't, and that meant I reached the kitchen a few precious seconds before he did, and was able to drop

Sadie so I could pick up the handset and desperately dial 9-1-1.

However, the operator was only able to say, "Nine-one-one, what's your emergency?" before Mark appeared in the kitchen, grabbed the phone from my hand, and tore it from the wall.

Or at least, I assume that's what he planned to do. But since the phone was bolted to a thick adobe wall and wasn't going anywhere, instead he just yanked the cord from the body of the unit, leaving him holding the handset and looking mildly foolish.

Not foolish enough to keep me from hurrying to the other side of the room, putting the kitchen island between the two of us. I didn't know whether that would be enough distance to really help, but I figured something was better than nothing.

"The police will be here soon," I said, glad to hear I sounded mostly calm. Maybe just the smallest tremor in my voice as I said "soon," but considering Sadie had started barking ferociously at Mark the second he pulled the phone from my hand, I doubted he'd be able to hear that bit of betraying unsteadiness.

"Shut that dog up," he growled, directing a baleful glance at Sadie, who was smart enough to stay close to me but who was now letting out a low growl that told me she wouldn't hesitate to launch herself at him if my intruder got too close.

If she'd been a Rottweiler or a pit bull, I might have thought I could rely on her to keep me safe until the police showed up...*if* they showed up, that is. I desperately hoped the operator had figured out something was horribly wrong at 11 Shadow Ranch Lane, but I couldn't bet on that, just as I couldn't bet that my little chihuahua mix was remotely threatening enough to keep Mark Lemmon at bay.

"She'll shut up just as soon as you leave," I shot back, and he sent a smile in my direction that wasn't much more than a baring of teeth. His blunt features were reddened with rage, making the thin-lipped smile look that much more menacing.

"Not yet," he said, and now his tone was calmer, as though he knew he had me cornered and figured he had plenty of time to do whatever he needed to do.

Which might not be too far off from the truth. Even if the 9-1-1 operator had acted immediately, it was still about a seven- or eight-minute drive from the heart of San Ramon, where the tribal police headquarters were located, to Calvin's and my home.

A whole heck of a lot could happen in that span of time.

I leaned down to pat Sadie on the head, immensely glad she was smart enough to stay close. If Mark Lemmon hadn't hesitated to casually slip poison into someone's drink, I hated to think what he'd do to a small, defenseless dog.

At least she'd stopped barking, though, and her growl now rattled low in her throat, almost inaudible unless you were standing right next to her the way I was.

"We still need to talk," Mark went on, his tone almost smug now, as if he thought the way Sadie had quieted down was somehow his doing.

"We have nothing to talk about," I replied. "Really, the best thing you can do is turn yourself in. I don't think threatening me is really going to help your case."

One eyebrow lifted at an amused angle. I'd been able to tell from the family photos I saw in his house that Mark Lemmon was a big man, over six feet, with broad shoulders and the kind of build that made him look like maybe he'd played football in high school or college. He had some middle-aged sag going on, with a definite spare tire around his middle, but he was still big enough to put me—and Sadie—through a wall.

No wonder his wife was so afraid of him.

"'Turn myself in'?" he repeated, still looking amused. "For what?"

"For the murder of Aaron Galloway," I said steadily. "You were angry that your wife kept giving money to someone you thought was a fraud, so when the opportunity to get rid of him permanently presented itself, you dumped some arsenic in his coffee and called it a day."

To my surprise, Mark actually chuckled. "You've got quite the imagination, don't you?" he said. "Must come from messing around with all those stupid Tarot cards and the other crap you sell in your store."

I bristled. I'd always made it a point not to mock other people for their beliefs even if they ran counter to mine, and so to hear this scumbag of a murderer and a domestic abuser sneering at my spiritual practices made my blood boil.

However, at least I had him talking, and the longer I could draw this out, the better the chance that someone would show up on my doorstep to investigate that aborted 9-1-1 call. "It's not my imagination," I said, although I knew my witchy intuition...and some input from my pendulum...was definitely what had guided me to the conclusion that he was the one who'd killed Aaron Galloway. "You had the means, and you had the motive. I'll let the police piece together the rest of it."

Mark Lemmon's mouth lifted in a very thin smile. "You really think I'm going to let you do that?" Without waiting for me to reply, he went on, "No, I think the problem will have taken care of itself well before then."

Before I could say anything, Sadie let out a warning bark, even as he lunged in my direction, moving faster than I could have imagined. Yes, the island was in the way, but he was about to close up the distance in just a second or two.

Desperate, I looked around for something I could defend myself with. Unfortunately, the knife block sat at the far end of the kitchen counter from where I stood, so I couldn't reach it even if I actually had the guts to stab someone…and I wasn't so sure I was capable of that kind of physical violence.

My gaze fell on the Instant Pot, though, which sat on the tile countertop less than a foot from where I was standing. Without even stopping to think, I grabbed the thing and yanked the plug from the wall, and then hurled the pot right at Mark Lemmon's head.

The appliance flew through the air and connected with the top of his forehead with a metallic clank. But although it smacked right into him, the Instant Pot probably wouldn't have finished the job…except that he stumbled, caught his foot on the rag rug in front of the island, and then pretty much took himself out by smashing the side of his head on a corner of the island's butcher-block surface as he fell.

He hit the ground with a thud, blood already trickling from the wound at his temple.

So much for that rug.

As I pulled in a breath—and wondered whether I should lean down to see whether my assailant was breathing as well, even if I really didn't want to get that close—Calvin's voice came to me from the living room.

"Selena, where are you? Are you okay?"

"In the kitchen," I said, now giving myself free rein to let my voice shake as much as I wanted.

Sadie gave a welcoming bark and ran to the kitchen entrance to greet her daddy, tail wagging and her ears up. Clearly, she thought everything was all fine now that Calvin was on the scene.

He came into the kitchen and stopped dead a few feet in as he caught sight of the man lying unconscious on the rug. "Did you do that?" he asked, tone incredulous.

"Well, sort of," I replied, then hurried over to him so I could take his hand in mine and reassure myself that I was okay, that I'd survived an encounter with a murderous intruder and lived to tell the tale. "I started it with the Instant Pot, and then he knocked himself out as he was falling."

Calvin hugged me tight for a moment, obviously wanting to reassure me—or maybe the both of us—that I was safe now and that I had nothing to fear. Still holding my hand, he walked over to look down at Mark Lemmon's limp form, then shook his head as he caught sight of the dented Instant Pot lying a few paces away, the heavy-duty plastic on the lid now cracked in several places.

"Who is that guy, anyway?" Calvin asked, clearly mystified.

I was a bit surprised he didn't recognize the man, but I reminded myself that my husband didn't have every single person in Globe memorized the way Josie did. "His name is Mark Lemmon," I explained. "He's the one who killed Aaron Galloway. I guess he found out I was on to him and came out here to shut me up before I said anything to Henry."

Calvin's mouth thinned. "Good thing he's unconscious," he said. "Or I'd knock him out myself. You can talk to Henry later about the whole Galloway thing, but right now, I've got plenty of reason to arrest the guy for aggravated assault. Of course, I'll need to call an ambulance first."

Which was what he did, using the police

walkie-talkie he had clipped to his belt rather than his cell phone. Luckily, my would-be attacker showed no signs of rousing as we waited for the ambulance to arrive, and good thing. Otherwise, Mark Lemmon would have been carted off to the hospital in handcuffs.

I rode with Calvin in his Durango, Sadie in my lap, as we followed the ambulance to the Cobre Valley Medical Center. He wanted to be there to read Mark his rights as soon as he regained consciousness.

Because Sadie wasn't a service dog, she wasn't allowed through the hospital's doors. In a way, that was all right, since it wasn't as though I'd be permitted anywhere near Mark Lemmon, not after Calvin informed the hospital staff that the man being wheeled in was a jail patient and all the proper security protocols needed to be in place to make sure he stayed put and didn't present a risk to anyone.

As I waited in the car, I held on to Sadie, realizing for the first time how much my hands shook. Yes, it had all turned out okay…but what if it hadn't?

I told myself not to borrow trouble. Mark had exposed himself as the bad guy he was, and now he would be going away for a very long time. In a way, I should be glad that he'd given in to his temper and come chasing after me. If he'd maintained his cool and not threatened me physically, it might have been a lot harder to prove his guilt.

After a wait of about twenty minutes, a span of time that would have felt interminable if I hadn't had Sadie there to keep me company as she sat on my lap and gave my hand a reassuring lick from time to time, Calvin came back to the Durango and slid into the driver's seat.

"He's awake," he said. "I read him his rights and told him Henry Lewis would be along in a bit to ask him some more questions. Of course, the guy started spluttering that he hadn't done anything wrong and you're the one who should be arrested for assault, but I just let him know that you were defending yourself in your home and no jury in this state would convict you. That shut him up...for the moment, anyway."

"Small blessings," I said with a faint little smile, and Calvin reached over to touch my arm.

"You okay?" he asked gently.

"I am now," I replied. "Let's go home."

As expected, Mark Lemmon vociferously protested his innocence, but no one was buying his claims that he was being wrongfully accused of Aaron Galloway's death, especially after

Henry Lewis got a warrant to search the man's home—including the garage—and found lab equipment that revealed traces of pure arsenic, a sure sign that he really had been synthesizing the poison in his home-grown lab. And because the judge denied bail—not that Nora probably would have paid it anyway—he got to cool his heels in jail until his court date rolled around.

To Chief Lewis's credit, he didn't wait for the lab results on the equipment seized from Mark Lemmon's garage to request that all charges against Josie Woodrow be dropped and that she be released immediately. This all happened late on Friday evening, long after a judge should have normally been around to adjudicate on the matter, but it sounded like Henry pulled a few strings, and once she was freed, she called her nephew Brett to come pick her up and drive her home.

That was probably why she was looking much more rested than the last time I'd seen her when she came breezing into the shop on Saturday morning a little after ten. Once again, I'd told Archie he could take the day off in order to be with Victoria…and allow them some extra rehearsal time before their competition that night. I hadn't breathed a word about their ball-room dance ambitions to anyone, not even Calvin, and I had to admit keeping that particular secret was just about killing me, mostly because I really wished a bunch of us could go to the tournament and lend my friends some moral support.

"Josie," I said, and came out from behind the counter to give her a big hug. "I'm so sorry I couldn't get you out of jail in time for Thanksgiving."

She waved away my concerns with an airy flap of her hand. "Nonsense, Selena," she replied at once. "I know you tried. Well, more than tried, since if it hadn't been for your expert sleuthing, I'd still be stuck in that awful cell."

I honestly didn't know how "expert" my investigation had been, since I'd mostly felt as though I was bumbling from one flimsy clue to the next, unsure as to whether any of it would add up in the end. "Still—" I began, and she shook her head.

"You only missed it by one day," she cut in, stopping my protests. "And Brett and Terry brought me some wonderful tidbits, so it's hardly like I missed the holiday at all. Also, Terry is making her famous turkey tetrazzini tonight with some of the leftovers, and that means I really haven't missed my favorite part of Thanksgiving at all."

It seemed my friend was determined to make the best of the situation, so I didn't bother to protest further. At least now we all knew that the right person was locked up—maybe in the same cell where Josie had been confined—and so we could all do our best to go on with our lives.

The real reason for her visit...well, besides doing her best to absolve me of any lingering guilt...was to fill me in on the rest of the story. No doubt she'd gone to see Nora Lemmon first, just so she could understand better exactly why her husband had gone off the deep end and slipped that poison into Aaron Galloway's coffee.

"She felt terribly guilty about it all, poor thing," Josie informed me after saying she'd visited Nora at her house a while earlier. "Said it was her fault, and that if she hadn't given all their money to Pastor Galloway, none of this would have happened."

"'*All* their money'?" I repeated, aghast.

"Well, all their savings," Josie replied. "A pretty hefty chunk, from what it sounds like. And when Mark found out, he went through the roof—told her she had to get a job to earn back everything she'd thrown away on that shyster." Josie's voice lowered as she went on, "Even with him locked up, I could see how frightened she is of him. Thank God the judge denied bail."

Yes, that was definitely a piece of good luck

for Nora, although I thought it only fair, since that same judge had also refused bail for Josie, who was clearly not a threat to anyone. "Did she say why Mark was at the revival at all, though? I mean, everything I've heard made it sound as though he hated Aaron Galloway and everything he stood for."

Josie nodded. "Nora told me she'd gotten special VIP passes to the event from Chelsea Haven because of her generous donations, although at first Mark said he had no intention of going. Then he changed his tune after Nora explained what an honor it was and how the passes the church had given them would allow them to go backstage."

Which I guessed was when he'd begun to formulate his plan to poison the pastor. I was sure Chelsea could have had no idea when she handed out those passes that she was inadvertently dooming her boss—and lover—to die by poison.

My friend must have thought the exact same thing, because she said, "I'm sure he only went because of the chance to get revenge on Pastor Galloway. The whole thing is terrible."

"It is," I agreed, thinking of all the lives which had been affected by that one terrible act of vengeance. "But at least Mark Lemmon is locked up now and won't get the chance to hurt anyone ever again. Did Nora say what she planned to do next?"

Josie's expression sobered. "Yes," she said. "She told me she wants to sell the house and move to Tempe or maybe Mesa so she can be closer to her daughters while they're in school, and she wants me to handle the sale. I think she'll make a good bit on the place, since they've owned it for years and they have a lot of equity. It might be enough for her to buy a condo free and clear, so, even though she'll still need to work, her overhead should be fairly low."

About the most positive outcome Nora could have hoped for. I found myself wishing her nothing but the best—she might have made a few mistakes, but she deserved a second chance in a place where she could start over and look forward to the next stage of her life.

"That's wonderful news," I said, and Josie brightened immediately.

"Yes, I think so, too," she replied. "And speaking of selling houses, I really need to get to my office. The work has been piling up ever since Henry put me in that darn jail cell."

I couldn't help smiling back at her. That was Josie, resilient to the core. Most people would have wanted to take the rest of the weekend off to recover from their ordeal, but not her. No doubt she'd clear up the backlog at her real estate office first and then head over to City Hall to tackle whatever business also needed attention.

"Then I won't keep you," I said. "Have a wonderful day—you've earned it!"

Her light blue eyes twinkled, and she said goodbye and headed out. As I watched her, I couldn't help shaking my head a little, even as I smiled.

It would definitely take a lot more than a false accusation of murder to keep Josie Woodrow down.

Calvin and I had our own meal of leftovers—smoked turkey flautas accompanied by a fresh batch of black beans and rice—during which I told him about my encounter with Josie, and what she'd learned from Nora Lemmon. He seemed glad it was all going to work out for Nora, although he shook his head over the extreme measures Mark had taken to deal with the loss of their savings.

"Sounds like he should have gone to marriage counseling instead of poisoning the guy," Calvin remarked, then ladled some more black beans onto his plate.

"I don't think Mark was the kind of guy to see a marriage counselor," I replied, "especially when you remember he liked to use Nora as his punching bag."

My husband didn't exactly wince, but his mouth thinned a bit. He was the type of man who wanted to make sure everyone was safe and protected, and the thought of a woman having to endure that kind of abuse probably made him far angrier than his current calm demeanor would indicate.

"You're probably right," he said, but didn't add anything after that, telling me he really didn't want to pursue the subject further.

Which was fine by me. Nora had suffered horrors I honestly couldn't imagine, but it sounded as though she was getting her life back on track and had a lot to look forward to. As for Mark blaming her for their money troubles, well, one could probably have argued that if it weren't for the way he'd made her bear the brunt of his anger and frustration for the past decade or so, she might not have turned to Life Springs Church and Pastor Galloway for comfort.

Later that night, just after we'd turned off the TV and were about to start getting ready for bed, my phone pinged. I picked it up, frowning faintly, since pretty much everyone knew not to contact me after ten o'clock unless it was some sort of dire emergency.

In this case, however, I was more than glad of the interruption.

We won! the message said, and I found myself grinning. Not that I'd had any real doubts, since I'd seen Archie and Victoria dance and knew they were amazing, but still, this was their first competition, and sheer nerves could have gotten in the way of their victory.

I should have known better. Seventy years as a cat had definitely taught Archie how to land on his feet.

"Who is it?" Calvin asked, expression curious. He knew as well as I did that I very rarely got text messages at that hour of the night.

"Archie," I said briefly, then added, "I'll tell you about it in the morning."

My husband still looked puzzled, but he didn't press me for more information. "Okay, we can talk about it over bacon and pancakes."

I went on my tiptoes and pressed a kiss against his lips. "It's a deal."

We got ready for bed after that and then snuggled together in the big king-size bed, Sadie curled in her usual ball just past my feet. Soon enough, Calvin's breathing became rhythmic, telling me he was fast asleep, and I let out a satisfied breath.

It was good to know he'd be there tomorrow morning…and every morning to follow.

Once again, all was right in my world.

The End

Selena's adventures will continue in *Ballroom Bits*, releasing in April 2023.

Also by Christine Pope

LATTES AND LEVITATION

(Cozy Mystery/Paranormal Romance)

Caffeine Before Curses

Muffins After Magic

Pastries and Prophecies (March 2023)

UNEXPECTED MAGIC

(Urban Fantasy/Paranormal Romance)

Found Objects

Finders, Keepers

Lost and Found

Finding Destiny

HEDGEWITCH FOR HIRE

(Cozy Mystery/Paranormal Romance)

Grave Mistake

Social Medium

Household Demons

Perpetual Potion

Jingle Spells

Wandering Monsters

Uninvited Ghosts

Prophet Motive

Ballroom Bits (April 2023)

THE WITCHES OF WHEELER PARK*

(Paranormal Romance)

Storm Born

Thunder Road

Winds of Change

Mind Games

A Wheeler Park Christmas

Blood Ties

Healing Hands

Wishful Thinking

Smoke and Mirrors

MISS PRIMM'S ACADEMY FOR WAYWARD
WITCHES*

(Fantasy/Academy Romance)

Misspelled

Dispelled

Expelled

PROJECT DEMON HUNTERS*

(Paranormal Romance)

Unquiet Souls

Unbound Spirits

Unholy Ground

Unseen Voices

Unmarked Graves

Unbroken Vows

THE DEVIL YOU KNOW*

(Paranormal Romance)

Sympathy for the Devil

Charmed, I'm Sure

A Wing and a Prayer

Wish Upon a Star

THE WITCHES OF CANYON ROAD*

(Paranormal Romance)

Hidden Gifts

Darker Paths

Mysterious Ways

A Canyon Road Christmas

Demon Born

An Ill Wind

Higher Ground

Haunted Hearts

THE WITCHES OF CLEOPATRA HILL*

(Paranormal Romance)

Darkangel

Darknight

Darkmoon

Sympathetic Magic

Protector

Spellbound

A Cleopatra Hill Christmas

Impractical Magic

Strange Magic

The Arrangement

Defender

Bad Blood

Deep Magic

Darktide

THE DJINN WARS*

(Paranormal Romance)

Chosen

Taken

Fallen

Broken

Forsaken

Forbidden

Awoken

Illuminated

Stolen

Forgotten

Driven

Unspoken

THE WATCHERS TRILOGY*

(Paranormal Romance)

Falling Dark

Dead of Night

Rising Dawn

———

THE SEDONA FILES*

(Paranormal/Science Fiction Romance)

Bad Vibrations

Desert Hearts

Angel Fire

Star Crossed

Falling Angels

Enemy Mine

———

TALES OF THE LATTER KINGDOMS*

(Fantasy Romance)

All Fall Down

Dragon Rose

Binding Spell

Ashes of Roses

One Thousand Nights

Threads of Gold

The Wolf of Harrow Hall

Moon Dance

The Song of the Thrush

THE GAIAN CONSORTIUM SERIES*

(Science Fiction Romance)

Beast (free prequel novella)

Blood Will Tell

Breath of Life

The Gaia Gambit

The Mandala Maneuver

The Titan Trap

The Zhore Deception

The Refugee Ruse

STANDALONE TITLES

Hearts on Fire (Paranormal Romance)

Taking Dictation (Contemporary Romance)

Golden Heart (Gaslight Fantasy Romance)

Night Music: A Modern Reimagining of The Phantom of the Opera (Contemporary Romance)

Ghost Dance: A Sequel to Gaston Leroux's The Phantom of the Opera (Historical Mystery/Romance)

Flight Before Christmas (Fantasy Romance)

* Indicates a completed series

About the Author

USA Today bestselling author Christine Pope has been writing stories ever since she commandeered her family's Smith-Corona typewriter back in grade school. Her work includes paranormal romance, cozy paranormal mystery, and urban fantasy, among others. She makes her home in beautiful Santa Fe, New Mexico.

Christine Pope on the Web:
www.christinepope.com

facebook.com/ChristinePopeAuthor
twitter.com/ChristineJPope
pinterest.com/ChristineJPope
bookbub.com/authors/christine-pope